24
STORIES

24 STORIES

OF HOPE FOR SURVIVORS OF THE GRENFELL TOWER FIRE

Edited by Kathy Burke

Unbound

This edition first published in 2018

Unbound
6th Floor Mutual House, 70 Conduit Street, London W1S 2GF
www.unbound.com

Text design by PDQ

A CIP record for this book is available from the British Library

ISBN 978-1-78352-586-7 (trade pbk)
ISBN 978-1-78352-588-1 (ebook)
ISBN 978-1-78352-587-4 (limited edition)

Printed in Great Britain by Clays Ltd, St Ives Plc

1 3 5 7 9 8 6 4 2

Dear Reader,

The book you are holding came about in a rather different way to most others. It was funded directly by readers through a new website: Unbound. Unbound is the creation of three writers. We started the company because we believed there had to be a better deal for both writers and readers. On the Unbound website, authors share the ideas for the books they want to write directly with readers. If enough of you support the book by pledging for it in advance, we produce a beautifully bound special subscribers' edition and distribute a regular edition and ebook wherever books are sold, in shops and online.

This new way of publishing is actually a very old idea (Samuel Johnson funded his dictionary this way). We're just using the internet to build each writer a network of patrons. At the back of this book, you'll find the names of all the people who made it happen.

Publishing in this way means readers are no longer just passive consumers of the books they buy, and authors are free to write the books they really want. They get a much fairer return too – half the profits their books generate, rather than a tiny percentage of the cover price.

If you're not yet a subscriber, we hope that you'll want to join our publishing revolution and have your name listed in one of our books in the future. To get you started, here is a £5 discount on your first pledge. Just visit unbound.com, make your pledge and type **24** in the promo code box when you check out.

Thank you for your support,

Dan, Justin and John
Founders, Unbound

With special thanks to Jo Rowling and Gary Lineker for their generous support of this book.

CONTENTS

FOREWORD
PTSD Explained

DR DEAN BURNETT

Dean Martin once sang about what memories are made of. A fresh and tender kiss, one stolen night of bliss, one girl, one boy, some grief, some joy. Looked at this way, it sounds more like an elaborate recipe, perhaps something concocted by Heston Blumenthal. But despite the presumable lack of neuroscience qualifications held by Dean Martin or the original writers of the song, it's a surprisingly accurate portrayal of the diversity of human memory.

I specify human memory because the word 'memory' is very common these days but often used more in the technological sense. The memory on your phone, your laptop, your hard drive, your SD card or USB drive. While there are some overlaps between the technological and biological ways that memory is processed, there are also many considerable differences. The memory on your phone or laptop is essentially a huge blank space into which useful information can be inserted and retrieved at will, and the files and documents you put in will (hopefully) be exactly the same when you retrieve them for use later.

A lot of people seem to think that the human brain operates on similar principles, passively absorbing the information we take in from our senses and storing it in a useful form for later retrieval and use. However, this is far from the case. Our brain isn't some passive recording device that just logs anything and everything we show it. For one, this is technically impossible. Despite our brains regularly being portrayed as awesome, powerful objects beyond our understanding, the truth is that, for all their undeniable complexity and capabilities, they're still physical organs, so are subject to physical and biological limits like any other. The laying down of memories depends on the brain forming new connections – synapses – between neurons. This takes time and energy and resources, and the limits of biology means the brain doesn't have boundless reserves of these things.

Consider how vivid our perception of the world is. Every second we receive a full panoramic experience of our environment, complete with sight, sound, smell, touch and taste. Life is high-def and multi-sensory. But, thanks to the limits of biology, to save every waking moment of this in precise detail is beyond the ability of the brain. What this means in practice is that our brain prioritises some memories over others; it has to focus on what's 'important' and disregard anything more trivial or inconsequential.

This is not something to be taken lightly either; our ability to function in our complex environment is dependent on the fact that our brain creates what is essentially a 'mental model' of how the world works. This is what our brains use to determine how we behave and react in any given situation. For instance, if you're sitting in a restaurant and you see someone walk past in just skimpy underwear, this would be very unusual – alarming, even. If you were on the beach, it wouldn't be. Such attire is normal and acceptable there. This is because your brain has this mental model of the world, and it includes the relevant information about how things work at the beach and in restaurants, and forms your expectations accordingly. But this mental model is based on all our knowledge and learning and experiences of the world, and all these things are stored in our memory.

Therefore, it's imperative to the brain that only 'important' memories get the time and attention available.

How does it do this? How does our brain 'decide' what's important to remember, and what's not? Given that our brain is 'us', you'd think we could just consciously decide what's important and what isn't. And we can, to a certain extent; if someone tells us a phone number or address, we can repeat it to ourselves over and over to retain it. But that's a lot of work, and we obviously don't do that with everything we remember. What happens is that the processes determining which memories should be prioritised and which should be ignored are largely subconscious, so are influenced by factors beyond our conscious control. One of these is that the more vivid or emotionally stimulating an event, the more significant it is to the memory system.

This makes a certain amount of sense: the more parts of the brain involved in experiencing something, the greater significance the memory takes on, because there are more elements involved in processing it and more connections to it that memory systems can work with. If something is emotionally stimulating and or substantially 'vivid', it occupies a lot of our brain, so can be remembered more easily later on.

Some argue that emotions evolved specifically for things like this, and that they're essentially a shortcut for the brain, cutting down the need for intensive thinking and cogitation. If you're presented with something dangerous, for example, you could study it at length and assess all the aspects of it, and slowly work out that yes, it is somewhat hazardous, or you could experience fear and leg it, saving your bacon for another day. The latter leads to survival, the former leads to extinction.

That our memory system is more influenced by stimulation and emotion explains a lot – like why learning important things for our exams is so difficult. You can read reams and reams of dry mathematical equations or historical events, and as important as it may be for an upcoming test, unless it invokes a stimulating, emotional reaction (and it will in some people, no doubt), your brain's memory system won't be especially bothered about all that. Hence you need to revise it over and over again, until the message gets through. But you go on your first holiday in years, or get into some scrapes with your friends, and these are the things you'll remember easily, because they come bundled with a lot of emotional and stimulating information.

That's all well and good if it's a happy experience. It's great to be able to remember your wedding day, or that time you scored the winning goal, or the birth of your first child with clarity and ease. These are the memories that we look back on fondly, year after year. But, of course, life isn't always a carefree skip through the tulips. Bad things happen, we face hardships and dangers and threats all the time, even if the modern human has tamed the world to the extent that present-day threats are more nebulous and theoretical: losing your job to the recession, rather than losing a limb to a wolf.

Dangerous or threatening things trigger the brain's threat-detection system, which essentially scans all incoming information and spots whenever something could prove a hazard to us in some way. When we experience a danger or threat, this system invariably triggers the fight-or-flight response, that well-known adrenaline rush where we tense up, the blood drains from our skin, our focus narrows, our heart starts pounding, and so on. This is a deeply entrenched mechanism in our bodies and brains: it's kept us alive for the lifetime of our species and beyond, so it's hard to avoid.

If our threat-detection system picks up a minor or potential threat, it causes the release of precursor hormones like cortisol, which sort of prime us to engage in fight or flight if the threat becomes more prominent. This makes us tenser, flightier, more irritable. This is stress. Stress is OK when we're dealing with real hazards, but because humans have the ability to recognise more theoretical issues and have created this complex world where we're bombarded by them constantly (career, relationship, financial, political, environmental and many other complex, abstract problems that are a daily occurrence for most), we can easily end up in a situation where we experience stress in a chronic, persistent manner.

If you're stressed about losing your job because of uncertainty at the top of the company, what can you do about that? Not much, except wait it out, but it means that the source of the stress is persistent, constant, enduring. The stress chemicals are coursing through our brains and bodies all day, every day, and that's damaging for our health, both physical and mental, because our bodies aren't meant to be dealing with stress all the time. They can change, adapt and adjust, but often in harmful ways.

There are many short-term fixes for stress, like eating high-calorie foods or drinking alcohol to shut down the more worrisome parts of your brain, so people who experience persistent stress do these a lot. But these then have very negative effects on your health in turn, so your ability to function normally suffers further, which is in itself stressful, so you need to compensate for that, and the cycle goes on and on.

And that's just with relatively low-level, if persistent, sources of stress. When it's something big, like a major trauma, then it's far more intense on every level, particularly when it comes to the brain. When we're in the midst of a seriously stressful episode, be it an assault, a car crash, in battle, or whatever, our senses get knocked up several gears, any peripheral distractions get shut down, adrenaline and all the related reaction chemicals are flowing through our veins, and all the rest. One consequence of this is that our experiences are suddenly far more intense and vivid, given all the resources being shunted towards our senses and the related processing. They say time 'slows down' when you're under extreme stress, and in a way, it's true. Every element is suddenly much richer and more substantial; things that would barely be noticed in normal conditions are now crystal clear. It may be less than ten seconds of experience, but it's much denser and detailed than any other ten seconds you've ever lived through, so there's 'more' of it, and thus it feels as if it lasts longer. The brain is funny like that.

This is reflected in the memory system; events experienced during a traumatic, stressful, life-endangering event are extremely vivid and highly emotional, so the memory system has a lot to work with, and memories of said event end up being extremely pronounced and detailed as a result. Some refer to them as 'flashbulb' memories, implying that they're as rich and detailed as a snapshot of the incident. Studies suggest they aren't that detailed and thorough, but they feel as if they are, which is sort of the point.

You can see how our brains having such a setup would be useful for survival. When we're confronted by life-threatening dangers, we don't actually know what's going to happen; it's important not to miss anything about the situation, so our senses are ramped up. And should we be lucky enough to survive the incident, we certainly don't want to forget anything about it in case we're confronted by it again, so our memory processes follow suit. It's a good way to survive and then avoid dangers.

The trouble is, though, our big hefty brains are sometimes too good at forming and retrieving memories. Sometimes the memory of an extremely traumatic experience is so detailed and complete that it's almost, if not exactly, as traumatic as the event itself.

Every time you recall the memory it's like reliving it, meaning you experience the same feelings and emotions and stress that you did at the time. That's where we get post-traumatic stress disorder. Those who live through extremely traumatic events don't just get to count their blessings and carry on as before; the event stays with them, and they often end up reliving it over and over again. Some people can slowly get over it and come to terms with what happened, but sometimes every remembering of the event is like ripping the scab off a wound, making it fresh and painful all over again.

This obviously has huge knock-on effects for the everyday lives of the victims. They will, perhaps subconsciously, avoid anything associated with the event, be it a place, object, person, or whatever. Mood is much harder to lift when a horrific experience is constantly being thought of again and again. Levels of stress are much higher, stemming from the memories of the event like the ooze from an infected injury. It also means your mental model of how the world works is compromised. Everything you think of and anticipate is now coloured by the harrowing experience that nearly cost you your life; it ends up being factored in to your every thought and prediction, causing further stress.

Your comforting self-serving delusions are no longer useful: you've experienced mortal peril first-hand and know how real it is. You can no longer tell yourself 'it won't happen', because it did.

The mental-health field also uses something called the stress-vulnerability model, which states that each person's brain is capable of handling a certain amount of stress before it loses the ability to function normally and has a psychological break, developing serious mental health problems. Those with PTSD are already dealing with a great deal of stress, so it wouldn't take much to tip them over the edge, making them unable to cope (again). This causes a lot of stress, and so on.

If you were involved in a serious incident and ended up with a steel spike buried in your thigh, nobody would expect you to carry on as normal. The pain and restriction alone would stop you doing anything until it was dealt with. PTSD is like having the spike jammed into your mind, rather than your leg. It's not a physical injury per se, but the pain and disruption are very real. And unlike a physical injury, you can't just pull the spike out and patch things up. We can't do that with memories. Not yet, anyway.

One of the most traumatic things to experience is the loss of a home. Even if it's just due to lack of money or a change in career, it can be a deeply stressful and upsetting time for anyone. But to lose it in violent, destructive circumstances is considerably worse. Our home is a big part of who we are, our identity. It's where we feel safest, where we keep our things, it's where we retreat to when the world gets too much. Losing it rips a good chunk of the foundations of our lives out from under us. The only things more important to us are our loved ones, those closest to us.

The survivors of Grenfell lost their homes, en masse, through no fault of their own.

Many of them lost friends and loved ones too, at the same time. They ended up with nowhere to go, no resources to fall back on, and at the mercy of a system that clearly didn't care and, from what we can see, still doesn't. Not to have some form of PTSD would be more than unlikely – it would be borderline miraculous. But, as is sadly always the case, the mental-health needs of the people of Grenfell, understandably, come second to the immediate needs of rehoming and rebuilding their lives. There are many ways to help deal with PTSD, from counselling to therapies to medications, but all these things cost money.

By buying this book, you've made at least some contribution towards making sure those who want it can get the help they need.

We humans are a social species, and our brains have evolved to encourage and facilitate this wherever possible. As a result, numerous studies have shown that a reliable way to reduce your own stress and improve your well-being is to help others. Hopefully you can take some comfort in knowing you've now done just that.

INTRODUCTION
On PTSD and 24 Stories

R. MARTIN

I have lived with mental ill health for the majority of my life, and after going through various unsuccessful prescriptive therapies for bipolar II and clinical depression over twenty years, it was a sudden viral attack in 2008 which profoundly altered my health for better and for worse. Too fatigued to maintain the hard protective shell, layers of shock, trauma and grief surfaced volcanically; no longer stuffed down, my history confronted me head on; it had me in a corner and I knew the only option I had was to open up and find the right help.

I was formally diagnosed with post-traumatic stress disorder (PTSD) in 2009 by a consultant psychiatrist specialising in post-traumatic disorders, and for the past nine years he and a colleague have worked with me to help process, reorganise, witness inner and outer changes, create a workable structure and give me the tools to create a happier life. It is a work in progress; sometimes I slide, sometimes I glide, but I'm always evolving.

My delayed diagnosis was the impetus behind this book. Literally minutes after expressing my desire to help the victims of the Grenfell Tower fire, I joined forces with Paul Jenkins and Steve Thompson to create this project; then the sudden and unexpected appearance of Kathy Burke, who volunteered to edit this book, saw the project manifest at such velocity we had little time to stop and think.

This entire project has been born out of a collection of like-minded people: Paul, Kath, Steve and I joined forces and supported each other to see the project through to completion. Sometimes it was enormously difficult for me, physically and psychologically. At times I wondered whether it might have been easier climbing the north face of the Eiger in stilettos, yet along with the hurdles came opportunities and connections because everyone involved in the creation of *24 Stories* shared a single, compassionate vision.

When witnessing man-made disasters such as the Grenfell Tower fire unfold, I – like many people living with PTSD – share an unfortunate bond with the victims. I recognise that for the majority of people, deep shock and trauma do not heal of their own accord and they don't fade naturally; if trauma is ignored, time will compress it, solidifying it, layer after layer. Though the circumstances may differ, the symptoms of trauma tend to follow a common trajectory.

Throughout *24 Stories'* remarkable journey over the past year, we have had advice and support from many wonderful people. At one point I was at my wits' end; I felt that giving up and walking away might be the only option to save myself. During a phone call with an associate, I asked, 'Why would someone with PTSD take on a project like this? It's going to finish me off!' She replied, 'It's because you understand and you care. It's because we all care.'

This project has proven that people do care; they care specifically about the psychological welfare of others, and they recognise the long-term emotional and neurological impact of events like the Grenfell Tower fire.

My journey won't end with the publication of this book. I hope to continue in some capacity to help others who suffer from PTSD.

THE LANGUAGE OF FLOWERS

NINA STIBBE

We moved from the town to the countryside after our parents divorced. Our plan to join in with village life was looking good in the early days, when a procession of curious villagers arrived with bunches of flowers. But we soon realised no one liked us. My sister blamed me for doing handstands up the wall. I blamed her for looking furtive, but it was my mother's habit of talking about cricket that caused the most trouble.

Our first visitor – a woman in a long tartan kilt – appeared in our kitchen and bellowed, 'Well-come to the village, well-come,' and handed over half a tree's worth of distressed lilacs.

The gesture should have seemed friendly, but the rusting lilacs said not. Through her smile she asked if any of us was going to fetch a vase. She pronounced it 'vayse'.

She ran the tap hard and started to arrange the barky stems in our big glass jug as if it were her house. My mother asked if she'd heard the cricket scores and the woman swung round and stared at her. 'There,' she said, 'they'll last a couple of weeks at least.'

When she'd gone, our mother told us, in future, to always take people's flowers and put them into water straight away, without being asked. Then she cursed the lilacs for being a bad omen and put the vayse outside the back door. A moment later, our dog sicked up what looked like a pair of tights. 'See!' said our mother, blaming the lilacs.

To prove it, she found her book *The Language of Flowers* and, flicking through, came to the truth about lilacs in the house. Nothing is so portentous as lilacs (especially white ones) in the house, it said, except a robin flying indoors. My sister and I pored over the book.

'Never give marigolds,' it said, 'for this means a desire for riches.'

It told us that flowers could mean anything from 'please don't tell' to 'a deadly foe is near' and that a flower's meaning should always be understood before they are given. Or else God only knew what you might start.

Another flower-bearing caller in those early days was the vicar's wife. She arrived flustered and held out a skinny bunch of spring anemones with bruised, oil-paint petals and juicy stalks wrapped in a limp page of the *Herald*.

On the ball this time, I plopped them straight into water. The vayse being occupied, I used a milk bottle, which was a bit too tall, and the flowers looked as though they were trying to keep their heads above water so as not to drown. It was stressful because the vicar's wife seemed puzzled by my handling of the situation and never stopped frowning.

The vicar's wife had bad news and good news. Our mother would not be permitted to join the Mother's Union on account of being divorced. On the other hand, she'd be very welcome to help with the Bring and Buy, which occurred on the first Sunday of the month, after Holy Communion.

We consulted *The Language of Flowers* and discovered that the anemones stood for 'abandonment' and/or 'lust forsaken'. But my mother said we could ignore the meaning because the vicar's wife had probably just swiped them off someone's grave.

In response to that, the poor anemones slipped down into the milk bottle and were dead by teatime.

More visitors arrived. They'd hand over their primroses, take a look at us and scurry away – their worst fears confirmed.

'Why does everyone keep bringing flowers anyway?' I asked. 'We've run out of vayses.'

'They just want an excuse to come and have a look at us,' said my mother, 'and they've all got gardens full of flowers.'

'It's country life,' said my sister. 'In town they'd bring biscuits.'

A month or two later, an enormous bouquet of chrysan-themums in rusty orange colours arrived with the Dents, a couple who lived just around the corner. The husband, Jim, was quiet, but the woman, Ramona, was talkative and said, 'Good luck in your new home.'

'It's not that new any more,' my sister said and plopped the flowers into an earthenware jug. I offered tea, coffee or Ribena. The husband declined but Ramona went for a hot Ribena.

While we waited for the kettle to boil, my mother brought up the cricket, which pleased Jim but annoyed Ramona because she couldn't join in. My mother noticed her annoyance but made matters worse by asking for help with the crossword, and again Jim was keen, but Ramona not, and they put their two heads together over her newspaper and talked gibberish for at least five minutes.

Ramona stood with her hands on her hips. I'd opened the book and looked up the meaning of the chrysanthemums. Orange ones weren't listed, I told Ramona, but red ones meant 'I love you' and yellow ones meant 'dejection'. Ramona couldn't have cared less and looked at me as though I was stupid.

'My mother likes to know what flowers mean,' I explained, flashing the book's cover.

'Does she?' said Ramona.

'Yes,' I said.

'I expect she gets lonely without a man around,' she said, and my mother overheard and said, 'Yes, I do.'

The petals soon began to fall off the crysanths in clumps.

Like everyone else in the village, we had a garden full of plants and because flower-giving seemed to be the done thing, I began taking little bunches to my teacher. It started in the autumn term with a bunch of holly (foresight) and heather (good luck), and then a stem of jasmine (friendliness) and the teacher seemed pleased. I felt popular and welcome and soon it seemed terribly important that I arrive at the start of each week with a little floral offering. I'd pick them before breakfast and quickly check their meaning in the book so as not to accidentally tell my teacher she was about to die or run away to sea.

I really hit my stride in the spring though, and one day my bunch of daffodils (regard) in a peach tin so pleased my teacher that she built our whole school week around them. We sketched them, we read William Wordsworth's daffodil poem and wrote our own stories and learned about bulbs and growth.

I took in dwarf narcissi (self-esteem), bobbly grape hyacinth (modesty, sincerity), a couple of dandelion leaves (not listed), a clump of forget-me-not (faithful, true love) and a frond of euphorbia (not listed) and would take them to my mother to assemble into a pretty bunch and tie in a piece of orange bale twine and put into a jam jar.

In the early summer I might pick a floppy, open pink rose (grace and joy), some cow parsley (weed), the odd poppy (imagination) and all sorts of dangly, whispery grasses, dusty buttercups, even an ear of green corn. I always presented them as if from my mother. 'My mother sent you these from the garden,' I'd say, keen to enhance her reputation. And there they'd be, on the teacher's desk, dropping the odd petal, cheering us all up until Friday after lunch, when they'd be ready for the bin and I'd rinse out the jar.

One June day, a classmate copied me and arrived with a bunch of sweet williams. The following day I told the teacher the meaning of them (grant me one more smile) and she was more pleased hearing that than having the actual flowers and asked me to bring in the book.

We must've been in the village half a year when my mother jackknifed the car and pony trailer in the lane beside our house, and no amount of revving and manoeuvring seemed to help. The more she inched forward and back, the tighter the angle became. Just when she was about to scream or run away and never come back, Jim – the quiet husband of Ramona (who'd had the hot Ribena) – suddenly appeared. He jumped behind the wheel, sorted out the vehicular crisis and even patted the roofs of the half-dozen or so cars queuing to get along the lane as they passed. In return my mother gave him a glass of whisky and, as far as the village was concerned, stand-up sex in the back of the trailer. And the next day someone left a bunch of white roses (secret love) at our back door.

The nicest bunch of flowers ever arrived a few weeks after Jim and the jackknifed trailer. These were multi-headed white daisies with yellow middles, foliage all around and wrapped in doily paper. To my young eyes it was a true bouquet that you might only get from a proper shop and then walk along with people casting admiring glances at it and wishing they were giving it (or getting it).

The bouquet of daisies (loyal love, purity, faith) arrived at teatime one day in the hands of a well-dressed black man in a trilby and a brown suit who smelled of TCP. His name was William Thomas and he had an arrangement to meet my mother. It was the first we'd heard of it, but I put him at the kitchen table. My sister took the daisies, unwrapped them and put them politely in a vayse. I made him a cup of tea and asked how he was (fine) and ran up to alert my mother. She was in bed after a late night and needed time to get dressed.

William Thomas is here for your arrangement, I told her. 'Who?' she asked.

'William Thomas,' I said, 'he's come to our village on two buses, all the way from Trinidad, but he'll soon have his own car.'

My mother came into the kitchen eventually, just as William Thomas was finishing his tea. He'd come to our village on two buses, he told her. But would soon have his own car. She said she'd heard as much.

'The thing is, William, I don't know who you are or why you're here,' said my mother. 'Is there something I've forgotten?'

'I'm William Thomas,' he said, 'you answered my advertisement in the *Leicester Mercury*.' He fumbled in a secret jacket pocket, unfolded a page, tapped it and passed it to her. It was a typed letter. My mother read it and blinked rapidly. She handed it back to him.

My mother hadn't answered his advertisement. It's not something she'd have done and then forgotten. Someone had answered on her behalf and William Thomas had crossed the county on two buses to have a romantic date and to talk about cricket and flower meanings (as suggested in the letter) and would now have to get two buses back again.

My mother told him as kindly as she could that someone must have answered the advertisement on her behalf.

'But why would they do that?' William Thomas asked.

'I don't know,' said my mother.

'Because they don't like her,' my sister said, 'because she's having sex with their husband.'

William Thomas still seemed not to understand (I didn't understand) and neither my mother nor my sister had the heart to explain it.

William Thomas picked up his trilby and left.

With him gone, my sister felt she could tell me why and how this situation had arisen and what it all meant.

'It was just a cruel trick,' she said.

'On who?'

'On Mum,' said my sister.

'Not on William Thomas?'

'No, he was just a casualty of the trick,' she said.

'If it's a cruel trick on you and he's a casualty, why didn't you go on a date with him and talk about cricket?' I asked my mother.

'She can't,' said my sister. 'Jim Dent wouldn't like it.'

'What's Jim Dent got to do with it?' I asked.

I rode my bike to the bus stop and saw William Thomas standing there reading a small book, which I assumed was a *Wisden* but could have been a Bible. Buses came at a quarter past the hour. It was ten to.

At home again I told my mother William Thomas was standing at the bus stop looking dejected and out of place and people were staring at him – which they were. My mother was upset. She read the letter again and looked at the flowers. After a while she sent me to see if he was still there. He was.

We got into the car, picked up William Thomas from the bus stop and drove him into town. He sat in the front.

'Did anyone else answer your advertisement?' my sister asked.

'Yes, two nice ladies, but I didn't think I'd get along with them as well as your mother,' said William Thomas, twisting round to look at us. 'They didn't mention cricket.'

'You should try one of them next,' I said.

William Thomas agreed. 'Yes, I will,' he said.

We pulled over near St Margaret's bus station and William Thomas talked glowingly for a while about the bowling skills of Lance Gibbs. My mother joined in and brought up the left-handedness of her favourite, Gary Sobers. The two of them chatted like that for a while until William's bus was due and he got out of the car.

'Goodbye,' he said, leaning in, 'it was very nice to meet you all.'

We watched as he walked away with his hat in his hand. My mother rested her head on the steering wheel for a while, I suppose because of the cruelness of the world, and I thought for a moment she might jump out of the car and run after him, but she didn't.

I worried at the thought that you could be a casualty of someone's trick on someone else. *How could you guard against such a thing?* I wondered.

A TODDLER COULD DO ENGLAND

PAUL JENKINS
For Josh

It was all Japan's fault. Japan was the easiest.

Once you'd done Japan, then you were duty bound to try Poland. Piece of piss, Poland. England was easy too. A toddler could do England. Once you'd mastered them three, you could move on to other countries. Russia and China were tricky, but possible, providing you had mustard or piccalilli.

Actually, now he thought about it, it was all his dad's fault. Picture the scene: the summer of 1980. Ten-year-old Martin Monkhouse is watching the Olympics on telly with his dad, Fat Tony. Everyone knew Fat Tony. Fat Tony the postman. Fat Tony, who on Saturday afternoons got the train up to south London to watch his beloved Crystal Palace. Fat Tony, who would have eight or nine pints in the Selhurst Arms before the match and take his T-shirt off and do his famous war dance in the pub, shaking his big flabby torso all over the place whilst being serenaded with 'You Fat Bastard' by all the other mums and dads. Not Fat Tony who ran the taxi rank out Selsdon way, not that fat bastard.

Where was his dad now, eh? thought Little Martin as he stood behind a huge screen waiting to do a press conference. The nation demanded answers and Little Martin was going to have to fly solo.

Anyway, summer 1980. Little Martin and Fat Tony are on the sofa watching sport on telly. This is what they do every Saturday night when there isn't a home Palace match. Tonight they are watching the Moscow Olympics. Fat Tony wants Little Martin to love sport as much as he does. Ever since Little Martin could crawl, they've played in the garden together or the front room, recreating what they've just seen on the telly. Fat Tony as Big Daddy and Little Martin as Rollerball Rocco after the wrestling's been on. Look at them coming in, Little Martin covered in grass stains and his dad bleeding from the nose and laughing like a madman. Fat Tony is Pat Jennings in goal and Little Martin is Vince Hilaire. Goal! One-nil to the Palace!

The previous evening they had been in the garden; Little Martin had been Seb Coe in the 1,500 metres. And Fat Tony had been Steve Ovett. Tonight, though, it's raining and the Olympics are on cos Fat Tony's wife, Denise, is out with the girls watching a romantic comedy starring Dudley Moore at the local Odeon. It's the weightlifting on the telly. There's no British athlete involved, so Fat Tony is weighing up the competitors to see who he's going to get behind. There's only three left: two Russians and a Japanese bloke. The Russians, well, they might have been on our side in the war, but they aren't now, so that's them out. On this basis, and the fact that Tony has recently bought a brand new video recorder made by Toshiba, it is the short, fat little Japanese fellow that they plump for.

Hidetoshi Yakamoto. The commentator tells the viewers back home that Mr Yakamoto is a maths teacher from Nagoya.

'Blimey. You wouldn't be late with his homework, would ya, eh?' Fat Tony ruffles his son's mousey-brown hair with his fat fingers.

'No way, Dad. He's massive.'

'Course, the other two are bigger still. Russians, see. Probably got all mad KGB steroids in them to make them bigger than most blokes. Probably going to get shot if they don't win.'

'I don't want anyone to get shot, Dad.'

'Nah, I'm only joking. Shall we cheer on that little Jap fella, though, eh? He's on his own. Them Russian blokes can at least cheer each other up. Who's that Japanese fella got, eh? No one. He's on his own.'

Fat Tony paused to belch, putting down the can of lager on the arm of the sofa.

'He's on his own,' he continued. 'He's our man.'

Twenty minutes later, seemingly inspired by the Monkhouse support, the maths teacher from Nagoya was victorious over the Russians. This was cause for celebrations in Maidstone and Moscow.

Fat Tony loved to eat. He was a champion eater, and the kitchen was his arena.

'Fancy some bacon sarnies, Martin?'

'Yeah. Go on, then.'

'Do you want sauce?'

'Yeah, please.'

When it came to putting ketchup on the sarnies, both Fat Tony and his son were traditionalists. Slam it all over. But that was before the sight of the Japanese flag stirred something in both father and son.

The Land of the Rising Sun was triumphant and the Japanese flag stood proud above the austere Soviet gymnasium. Fat Tony stared at the four slices of white bread beneath him on the breadboard, his ketchup bottle poised above them.

With love and care, Fat Tony positioned the bottle and

gave its bottom a firm tap. An almost perfect red circle hit the centre of the bread.

'Hey, look, son. Japanese flag bacon sandwich!'

At this, they both started to laugh. Martin took the ketchup from his father and made a similar flag on his bread. They ate noisily and happily, and for the rest of the Olympics, used a variety of sauces and accompaniments to make flag sandwiches to celebrate any Olympic victory. On the Monday, Fat Tony came home very excitedly with a poster depicting all the countries of the world and their respective flags. Up it went on the kitchen wall, ready for condiment-based reference needs. These were the golden memories of Martin's childhood.

Throughout his teens, Martin looked forward to World Cups and Olympics as much for the flag sandwiches as the sport itself. His dad, too, loved these shared moments, and thought of his own strained relationship with his father as a boy. The only flags being waved in Fat Tony's childhood were white ones.

Some years passed. Martin left school for a stint at a local catering college. Fat Tony got sacked by the Post Office for not being small enough to fit into a Post Office-approved shirt. He stuck his last pay packet into the purchase of a fully equipped burger van. He bought a load of meat from Billy Banks, who'd just come out of Brixton nick for biting off the nose of a bookmaker at Catford dog track. The van was painted with the legend 'Fat Tony's Meat Wagon'. Monkhouse and son were in business.

June 1996. London. The European Football Championships are in town. England are playing Switzerland in three hours' time. The England team coach is slowly moving up the Edgware Road. On board, Mickey Sweet, England's charismatic Cockney captain, is trying to contain his nerves. Twenty years in the game and still the butterflies in the stomach. Still the aching sense of not being good enough, of not belonging. The nagging voices in his head he has learned to control, to ignore. Except for one.

Around Mickey, a group of likeable athletic millionaires are engaged in a harmless if somewhat tuneless singsong. It almost helps to drown the voices out.

Mickey stares out of the window. Two hours till kick off and already the roads are packed with supporters making their way. Through thick and thin, they come. They always come. *Why?* thinks Mickey. Anyone could do England these days.

Fat Tony and Little Martin are ensconced in a burger van parked close to Wembley Stadium. The national team coach drives slowly past and Fat Tony and Little Martin cheer loudly as they strain to see through the tinted windows.

Ninety thousand football supporters, and half of them coming past Fat Tony's Meat Wagon twice in the next few hours. Business is going to be booming.

There's plenty of competition though, and business isn't as good as it could be until, in the hours leading to England's crucial game with the Netherlands, Little Martin, inspired by all the St George's flags being dragged towards the stadium, resurrects the flag sandwich. Big slices of white bread quartered with the red cross of St George. Flagwiches. Two quid. Although neither of them know quite what this means, it becomes clear to many that Fat Tony and Little Martin have captured the public's imagination.

Overnight, the demand for flagwiches becomes phenomenal and just as the England team suddenly find themselves playing to their full potential and looking like world beaters,

Monkhouse and Sons find themselves making thousands of pounds a day more than they could have hoped for. One night, they're the jokey, cheer-you-all-up-after-the-bad-news item at the end of *News at Ten*. Suddenly Monkhouse and Sons are talking media rights and licensing money over a mobile phone they've seemingly acquired from nowhere.

By the time England lose to Germany in the semi-finals, Fat Tony's Meat Wagon is a household name. Richard Branson's invited them over to his island for drinks and Robert De Niro wants to buy the rights to the film of their life story.

From here on, every England football campaign was the cue for another launch of everyone's favourite fan-snack. Beckham Cross Buns in '98. Rooney Rolls a decade later. People could make them at home, of course, with just a bit of ketchup and bread, but it didn't taste like the ones you could buy during the World Cup from any participating store. What's more, it felt like sacrilege. England's astonishing win over the Dutch was a direct result of Little Martin artfully quartering a slice of cheap white bread with two lines of red ketchup.

'I mean, they really tapped into the zeitgeist, didn't they? They were like, the twelfth player in the team,' said David Bowie's nephew on a television show called *1996 Was Ace*.

'For me, there was a definite synergy between the smooth, symmetrical nature of the ketchup on the white bread and the movement of the white shirts. It was, dare one say it, a piece of postmodern psychic bonding, which acted as a kind of dress rehearsal for the post-Diana displays of public grief,' said a previously highly respected professor of poetry on *The South Bank Show*.

Twenty-one years later and Martin Monkhouse stood on the balcony of his expensive Thameside apartment looking out over the rainy evening. His dad paced anxiously inside as England failed to respond to the carefully timed launch of their latest business venture, Fat Tony's Brexit Butties.

'I'm going for a walk,' said Fat Tony as England let in yet another rubbish goal.

'Where you going? It's pissing down; it's only a game. It'll be all right,' said Little Martin.

It wasn't all right, though, and Little Martin knew it.

All across England, the final whistle prompted swearing at television sets, kicking of dogs and half-hearted suicide attempts. A property developer in Devizes decided that the agonising nature of England's defeat was just typical of his own life: so close to getting what you want and then blowing it right at the end. This idiot, a property developer called Trevor Ferris, decided to drink a bottle of black sambuca and swallow a load of painkillers to say goodbye to a life he considered wretched. However, Trevor forgot to take the painkillers along with the sambuca and got blind drunk, woke up feeling unwell, tripped over his cat and fell through his kitchen window and ended up paralysed from the neck down. Had he not decided to save a few quid on the windows, he wouldn't even have smashed them. Still, funny old game, eh?

Back in London, the England manager, Mickey Sweet, decided to forego the post-match press conference and ducked out of the stadium through a fire exit. He was fucked, he knew that much. You didn't lose a game like that and expect to keep your job. The papers were going to crucify him. The last manager but one – blimey. His team drew against Rwanda in the World Cup. Now, admittedly, Rwanda weren't a bad side, but you know, England were expected to win. Anyway, the erstwhile manager woke to find the headline 'Rwanka' over the front of the *Sun* with his photo. Mickey wondered what he was going to wake up to, what terrible pun they were going to wrench out of the word Montenegro. Walking fast with his head down, he suddenly realised he was amongst thousands of wet and pissed-off football fans.

'Fucking useless. Montenegro? Where's that? Jesus.'

'Well, at least that twat's sacked now.'

'Hundred grand a week to be fucking useless. Bastards.'

Slipping down a side street, Mickey pulled his mobile out of an inside pocket. Ignoring the missed calls message on the screen, he decided to keep walking down various alleyways and side streets until he spotted a sign indicating a basement bar called Monty's. Checking he had his wallet, he decided that a few stiff drinks was the answer and casually descended the steel staircase beneath the city. There was a big screen in the corner of the bar showing various ex-footballer pundits trying to be analytical and neutral whilst capturing the mood of the nation at the same time by offering their opinion as to who should be the next England manager. One of the pundits, a former international widely derided in his time as being a luxury player, was sticking the boot in, conveniently forgetting that the current man for the job was the same bloke he'd backed the last time round. As well as being his own brother.

'Family loyalties aside, he's let the nation down and he has to go,' said Terry Sweet.

Mickey struggled through a crowd to the bar, as no one seemed to be watching the television. Everyone was getting drunk, it seemed.

'A large Scotch, please,' he said to the barman.

The barman brought the Scotch, thanked him in an accent Mickey couldn't quite place and turned his attention back to the big screen. By now, the news was on the telly and everyone turned to watch. Little Martin was on the telly giving some sort of press conference. He looked devastated.

'Do you think you got the ingredients wrong, Martin?' said one reporter.

'Why didn't you stick with the flagwiches before such a crucial game?' asked another.

'Where's Tony?'

'I'm not sure. It's been a very difficult evening for everyone,' offered Little Martin by way of explanation.

At this point, Fat Tony walked into the bar. Spotting Mickey Sweet sat alone on a leather armchair, he rubbed his eyes in disbelief before grabbing a pint of lager and taking a seat next to him.

'Well, I've had better nights,' offered Fat Tony, introducing himself.

'I don't suppose ours can get much worse, though.'

'Might as well stay here and get pissed up, eh?'

And so, the soon-to-be sacked England manager and the managing director of the only flag-based snacks company in the world swapped autobiographies and anecdotes over a long night's worth of short drinks and tall stories. Had they been paying more attention, they would have noticed that they were drinking in the only bar in the whole of England aimed at the burgeoning Montenegrin community. Slowly the place filled with celebrating, disbelieving fans waving their flags and drinking heroic quantities of plum brandy. But they weren't paying any attention to that or to the telly that showed their faces in alternating close-ups throughout the night's news bulletins. Nor to the fact the complimentary crisps they were eating weren't just any old snack but traditionally baked burek, specially designed in the same colours as the proud Montenegro flags that danced around them.

SEVENTEEN-STOREY LOVE SONG

IRVINE WELSH

She was falling off the roof of a building in New York City. It was seventeen storeys high. To everybody looking over in horror, it was like a life going by. It started slowly and picked up speed as she receded from them. Now Melinda Pallister understood: how old people seemed to be lurching slowly to the grave, but that was only on the outside. Internally they were sprinting at breakneck velocity, or at least it must have felt like that, as, like now, the world uncompromisingly hurtled by in the opposite direction.

Melinda was accelerating to her death.

But inside her mind, as she flailed through the air, aware of the terrible space around her, everything had slowed down. She knew it was going to be some time before she hit the ground.

The hotel, in Greenwich Village, just off Sixth Avenue, was not one of Manhattan's architectural treasures. A drab, utilitarian 1980s construction, its main claim to fame was a small rooftop terrace with a pool and bar, which had become a cool go-to spot for socialising office workers. The DJs invariably played a heady mix of dance music to get bodies gyrating around the magnetic sapphire water as the cocktails took effect.

Melinda and her friends enjoyed drinking and flirting. She was finally embracing her recently achieved single status with verve. A suffocating romance had ended a few months back, but as so often happened in the city, economics had bonded her and Chad Davis together, against the will of both. Neither could afford to move out, and the next phase of their relationship had been a war of attrition over the occupancy of their rent-controlled apartment. This state of affairs had been highly detrimental to hedonistic and romantic pursuits. Then, in this strength-sapping battle of nerves, Chad had blinked first, going to visit his brother in Alaska. Melinda had struck, changing the locks, putting Chad's stuff into a storage facility, paid through their depleted joint account, and installing her friend Becky as roommate.

So a celebration was finally in order.

Melinda knew that, post-Chad, love would find her quickly. She was sought after by the lawyers and stockbrokers who covered weak chins and lantern jaws alike with the ubiquitous sensitive hipster beards, hoping it would soften the perception of professional abrasiveness and add the requisite soul and depth. Her incredibly long legs were her main assets. But these also meant that Melinda's centre of gravity was askew, as her hips were, when she stood on the slatted wooden seats, over the line of the aluminium banister topping the glass balustrade. She was up there to gain a better view, through the crowded deck, of Becky, who, in denim cut-offs and tank top, had audaciously jumped into the pool, to whoops and cheers. Then Melinda's heel had caught in between the slats and snapped off, sending her tumbling backwards. As she felt her ass rest on top of the banister, Melinda let out a confused but embarrassed smile before she then slid back in a sickening terror, witnessing her own demise in the wide-eyed and open-mouthed horror of her friends Ruth and Amanda as she groped at the air while falling back into nothing but space.

Then, as things slowed down, Melinda thought: *Shit*. There was so much to do. A promotion at the advertising agency, while not guaranteed, was a strong possibility. There were bills to pay – poor Becky – and her cat, Sparky; he would be fine with Becky. Chad would feel vindicated; his monstrous ego would reconfigure her death into a possible suicide occasioned by the loss of his love.

Other partners before Chad flashed through her mind, their faces kind and open. Trent. Gilmore, Ben, Bruce, Colin, Bret, Kurt ... she realised that they were all essentially the same. Suburban white boys, every one of them, since high school. She had once flirted with a black barman she wanted to go home with, but had backed down when he told her he got off at eleven. Then there was the time she made out with Armando, whose parents came from Puerto Rico, and of course there was Yanos, the older but creepily charismatic Polish doorman in the building, who looked at her in lust and made the odd suggestive comment. She'd wanted all those men. Why didn't she have them? She wasn't racist. Her parents ...

Marcus and Jill Pallister in Connecticut would be devastated. No parents wanted to outlive their offspring. Melinda was twenty-five, but her death would still be seen by them as emblematic of their failure to protect their child. Would their marriage even survive? Would they?

She thought back to Trent. He had been the one before Chad, and the best of the bunch. A genuinely nice guy, and it lasted eighteen months. She wasn't ready for his needy suffocation. Now she wanted those strong arms around her, arresting her tumble through space.

Melinda wished that the building had been absolutely massive: the bigger the better, perhaps two hundred storeys instead of seventeen. That way she would certainly die before the impact. Now she would be splattered onto the pavement below. Every bone shattered. Perhaps a breath still left in her broken body before it ebbed away. She braced herself for the concrete's demolishing impact.

What should have been her final moments wrenched her into confusion. Was this death? The impact was forceful enough; she felt her body beset with pain, as if her bones were being pushed through her flesh. But she was slowing down. Then she was airborne again, briefly, tossed to the heavens by some uncompromising force, flying like a drunk, a spreadeagled Superman, towards the apex of the hotel. But this ascent was only brief, as her still-mortal trajectory arched in gravity and her fall resumed, but from a lower height. She braced as she saw the fibreglass roof rush towards her, which she crashed through, falling onto a pile of mattresses.

Melinda lay on the soft bedding and looked up. There was whiplash in her neck, and some cuts on her arm. She laughed hysterically, until she froze over and burst into tears. She reasoned that her incredible journey had come to an end, not on the unforgiving pavement, but she had hit the canvas canopy above the hotel entrance and bounced into the road, catapulting through the flimsy roof of a parked truck.

Melinda wasn't sure how long she lay there – probably just moments – before the door was unlocked. Dan Chen, a small Korean man, stood before her. He was bringing the mattresses back from an industrial cleaning service in Queens. The rear delivery entrance had been blocked by another, larger, truck, one that was supplying fittings for the new kitchen in the downstairs restaurant area, and he'd been rerouted to the front of the building. Dan panicked when he saw the young woman lying on the mattresses. 'What happen? What happen here!'

Melinda looked at Dan intensely, then sucked down a huge breath and heard a command boom out from inside her, a voice she was now disinclined to silence: 'Shut the door! Come in and shut the door!'

Dan looked at her for a second, allowing himself to be briefly mesmerised by those long legs, then complied.

Melinda's friends Ruth and Amanda had taken the lift down to the street. They had seen no body when they looked over the parapet. Fitz Gilroy, the hotel's long-serving doorman, pointed in disbelief at the parked laundry van. Ruth and Amanda started banging on the door of the vehicle and fervently shouting her name.

But Melinda Pallister wasn't opening it. Not for a few minutes more.

THE GHOST OF JUNGLE

JULIAN GYLL-MURRAY

My world is one of change, of movement. People come during the day; others leave at night. Every morning, I wake up to abandoned tents flapping mournfully in the wind, enough waste strewn about them to fill the air with the hum of flies.

Sometimes people vanish before I get to say goodbye. At the borders of Jungle, there is a half-built church that a pastor deserted, forced as much by circumstance as anyone else. I go there sometimes. I pick my way through the mud and the detritus, and find the unfinished temple. I go through the door, and for a brief moment it is like entering home, but then I see the holes in the roof spattering the floor with sun or rain and suddenly all the comfort from being in the Lord's House evaporates. I know my mother would pinch me hard for thinking this – but it makes me feel like God, too, was caught in the flow, the wash of humanity that brought us here and will one day flush us out.

This charge, this movement, makes everyone restless. People shift from one foot to another as they gaze upon the motorway stretching along the hill. We eye the traffic with suspicion and hope, following its progress with darting eyes.

Every night there is a tide of people who go there, marching silently towards the golden lamplight as if they were insects attracted by the glow. They become silhouettes, flitting about the cars, picking at the back of Lorries and crouching on the hard shoulder like animals ready to pounce. Mother makes a lot of noise when she is having a bad night, so in the morning I sometimes get up early to watch the tide come back in; I watch lines of men with drooping eyelids pick their way back to their tents, shoulders slumped with disappointment.

It was at such a time, when the sun was easing its way over the horizon and the orange glow of the motorway was being swallowed up into the sky, that I saw you first.

There are some parts of Jungle that are unofficially agreed upon as toilet space; the closest one is called Shit Hill, nicknamed by the Sudanese. That's where you appeared, standing in the middle of Shit Hill, looking at me.

I am like everyone else here: I move, I shift. My eyes spin back and forth, following Lorries to see whether they will be filled or keeping an eye out for the group of Kurd boys I don't like. So when I saw you there, standing on Shit Hill without moving so much as a muscle, I immediately knew that you were dead. Your stillness froze me: all I could do was watch you while the tide of homecomers swilled around me, creeping into tents, picking their way through mud and waste. No one else could see you; of that I was sure.

You were there for me, communicating something with your unshakeable gaze, urging, imploring.

You were wearing the dress in which I last saw you, all those countries ago. It was dripping wet, filthy. You were pale, too, and your water-flattened hair made your head look smaller than it should. You were still so calm, so settled. Our restlessness comes from the uncertainty, the feeling that we are spiders ready at any moment to be washed down the plughole. You had none of that.

You, my sister, were free from it. Perhaps that is what death is.

Freedom – and stillness.

For the next few days, I imagined ghosts everywhere.

I saw them in abandoned tents, collapsed onto the muddy floor with sagging skins and poles jutting out into the air like exposed bones.

I saw them at night, amongst the exodus of shadows clambering up to the motorway.

I saw them in the forests around Jungle, where people head at dusk to look for petrol stations and car parks to find vehicles to slip into.

But I never saw you.

As the week progressed, Mother had one of her bad spells, and I was left on my own. And so, hoping that you would visit me, I went further than I had ever been before.

I passed by a French class in a container, where a host of people bleated out sounds in an awkward, uncoordinated chorus. I passed by the tent of a bicycle repairman, where someone was haggling furiously, bent bicycle in hand. I passed by a van of volunteers, where people were being handed clothes and sleeping bags with varying degrees of excitement and relief.

And then I came across the cricket pitch. It was, of course, not a real pitch: it was simply a stretch of sand. But that was how I came to think of it in the weeks that followed.

There was a group of Afghan boys circling around, shouting excitedly as they delineated the edges of the pitch with stones and grabbing the bat and ball off each other in eagerness to get the game started. Another group of Somali boys were there as well, looking shy and quiet, but as I got there they were gradually being accepted into the game, with one Afghan miming the motion of bowling the ball to them.

I had never seen cricket before, so while I recognised it was some sort of sport, I was happy to sit at the border of the pitch and see what would happen. After a few minutes, they finally started to spread out along the sand to play, with the Afghan boys pointing out good places for the Somalians to stand. A boy holding the ball positioned himself at a bunch of sticks, which had been planted in the sand, and another, holding the bat, placed himself at another set of sticks. They both made very grand, ritualistic gestures, as if the game could not start without a certain amount of stateliness.

And then they played.

It was baffling to me at first, with a lot of quiet pauses followed by furious bursts of movement, accompanied by shouts in all these different languages I did not understand. The suddenness of these switches from silence to noise left me grinning and enthralled; with every throw of the ball, I had no idea what would happen next.

I was so enraptured that I did not notice for many seconds that one of the Somali boys was urging me to come and join their team.

I looked about; there were no other girls here. Would the boys really want me to play? I could tell that the situation had caught the attention of everyone else, and there was a lot of grumbling at the idea of my inclusion.

But as I contemplated what to do, the thought of you came to mind, and I realised that in some way, you had led me here.

Feeling encouraged, I got up to the sound of cheering and groaning. It was unlike anything that had happened to me since leaving home, and I found myself grinning from ear to ear as I plodded across the sand in my flip-flops.

I spent the next few minutes being prepped by the team, the Somali boys suddenly acting like they were experts in the game they'd just learned to play. We communicated in broken Arabic, which I'd picked up a little from passing through Sudan, and they made me practise the batting motion over and over again.

When I came up to bat, some of the boys on the pitch laughed. But it didn't matter, because the bat was so big and unwieldy that I found myself giggling too, and it was like we were laughing at the world together.

The Afghan boy took a few steps back, getting ready to bowl, and, as he did this, I caught a glimpse of you, at the border of the pitch, looking at me with that steady gaze, your dress dripping and darkening the sand.

I smiled, and was happy. And when the ball was thrown to me, I hit it with all my might, so that it arched through the air, leaping out of Jungle and into the sky.

I ran, my flip-flops flip-flopping, and laughed, my laughter going even further than the ball, so loud that I was sure that even your wet, dead ears could hear it.

I came back to play every day. I was better than many of the boys, and they liked using me as a way to tease each other. We would meet there in that stretch of sand, and play long, long matches, whiling away the afternoons.

Our cries of excitement drew children from different countries. Many of our group would go and never be seen again, but they would soon be replaced by Syrians, Kurds, Pakistanis or Iraqis. We communicated to each other by giving each other nicknames and shouting and pointing, but whenever the wicket was hit, the cries were universal, every language reduced to an utterance of joy or disappointment. I began to wonder if it was the same for those who went on the motorway at night; if they, too, had common expressions for whenever a Lorry was won or lost.

In the afternoons, I would trudge back home, going around the different huts and tents and cafés, and grimly think of Mother and the lecture she would give me for being away too long. Then, after Mother told me how dangerous my behaviour was, we would go and receive food, and if she was in the mood, we'd find some Eritrean neighbours and listen to their travel stories.

I heard it all in those evenings. I learned that everything was going to be fine, but also that we should never hope for too much. I was told firmly that we'd be better off finding a way to stay in France – but also that the Queen herself was going to make sure we were all welcomed into England.

People would offer their almost-made-it stories, and I liked them because they were full of drama, like the fishermen's stories back home but more exciting. They would talk of how some of their friends had managed to sneak into a Lorry in a petrol station just a day's walk from Jungle, but that by the time they'd got there, the police were guarding it. They would talk of how they'd heard of their friends walking into the tunnel itself, spending hours and hours with the rumble of the sea above their heads.

Sometimes someone would talk about home, but that always felt like a mistake: it would swallow up all the energy, all the fuel that people needed to carry on. There would be silence, followed by another almost-made-it story to reinvigorate us again.

Once the group looked to Mother and I, wondering whether we'd talk about our travels, or whether we had our almost-made-it story to contribute. But I knew that Mother would not want to talk, that it was too painful.

So I thought of you, and what you would do in such a situation, and decided that you would have made everyone laugh.

So I said that I did not have an almost-made-it story, because I *had* made it: I was the best cricket player in Jungle.

There came a day of particular turbulence.

The word spread fast, from one community to another. Once some of the Sudanese heard it, we were soon informed of it ourselves: Jungle was going to be evacuated and we were going to have to leave.

It was the kind of rumour that tended to surface every few weeks, but this one seemed to carry more weight than most. Walking through Jungle, I could sense a buzz, a mania, affecting everyone. I could hear more fights than usual, more crying. The group of Kurds that scared me were shouting at each other, apparently because of some violent incident with an Afghan gang the other side of the camp. Walking among the huts and the containers, I noticed that people were either huddled together in solidarity or breaking out into hysteria, packing and fighting over what they claimed was rightfully theirs. One group attacked a man so violently that he was pushed across three tents, squashing the fragile little homes into the mud. I even saw one group start to drag away their caravan by hand, and I wondered where they would go.

I rushed to find Mother to ask her what we were going to do. Was it finally time for us to catch a Lorry? Were we going to have an almost-made-it story for ourselves?

But it was no use. Mother was sitting in her tent, a blank, weak look on her face that I recognised immediately. The rumour, rushing around Jungle, had dealt her a blow, and she had been plunged into a bad spell. She needed time.

So I left again, weaving around the rushing people, the looting and the shouting.

Not knowing where to go, I went on my usual route which circled about the caravans with the scary men and led to the pitch. Sometimes, I had to clamp my hands over my ears, because there was so much anxiety in the air and the atmosphere was charged with anger. I wished I could close my eyes as well, but I did the next best thing and kept my gaze focused on the churned, muddy floor beneath my flip-flops.

At one point, there was a voice I recognised, spouting an incomprehensible language, and I could tell that some scary men were near, so I darted into a different alleyway of tents, and found myself in a patch of bushes.

I was hit by the smell: it was another Shit Hill. I gagged, and for a few moments did not realise that you were there too, standing in the bushes in front of me.

I had not seen you in a while, and my heart immediately made a leap. But, even more thrilling, you were close, so close that I could see all the little details of your face, so close that I could reach out and touch you.

We looked at each other for a bit. I gazed into your eyes, and you gazed into mine, and we comforted each other by having the same eyes we'd always had. Like a nervous child in front of an animal, I then tentatively put my hand forward, and you took it in your own. You were clammy, cold. Then I looked up from our hands and met your gaze again.

What is it? I breathed. What is it you want me to understand?

Slowly, slowly, you lowered your head, staring at the ground instead of me. I followed suit, and we looked at the little puddles you were making with the water dripping off you.

They filled pockets in the ground, then became dark circles as the water was swallowed down by the earth.

I did not see anything at first. But then it came.

In every puddle, for the briefest of moments before the water drained away, was an image. It was an image of the past, of the future, of dreams and of the world. There was smoke, and fire, and tears, and walking, and roads – long stretches of roads.

I looked up, and asked: is this what will happen, when Jungle ends?

But the moment I asked was the moment I realised that the answer was irrelevant. I glanced down: the puddles had been soaked up, and you weren't dripping any more. You were dry.

You stepped to the side, and pointed to a clearing ahead: the cricket pitch. There were a few boys there now, looking unsure as to whether to start a game or not. They were glancing at each other with worried looks, listening to the din of Jungle.

I smiled, and strode forward until I had penetrated the edges of the pitch delineated by stones. I reassured the others, like you would have. I told them not to listen to the sounds, not to watch the columns of smoke. I told them that we just needed to give the adults more time. No one spoke my language, but they understood anyway.

And so we started a match.

I played the best game of my life that day, and when I went back to the tent later I felt proud.

And so it was that I decided to speak to you every night, whispering in the dark while Mother sleeps her troubled sleep.

I will talk about what you taught me with your gaze. I will talk of all the change and movement that any day can bring. And I will tell myself to be stronger. I know, now, how to be strong, because of you, and because of that flat piece of sand in Jungle where I'd found my stillness, just like you had found yours.

A BRIDGE

DAN REBELLATO

The sound he can hear is water, rushing through the ship. It's sinking and the water is battering its way up through the ship, bursting the doors, pushing through the corridors, and it makes a sound like roaring. Like a water lion racing towards him.

The ship is on its side and the terrified passengers have made the corridor wall into a floor and they are trying to find an exit. The corridor is six feet wide, which means now it's six feet high, and he's six two, so he's hunching as he runs.

Is he scared? he wonders. What a question, he thinks. But, he observes, he always feels detached in moments like these. Moments like these? His wedding; he gave his vows, but he felt he was watching himself do it, like he was in a theatre, watching himself on stage doing the lines. I wish the women would stop screaming. Please.

The column of passengers stops. What's wrong? shouts a woman at the back. He puts his finger in his ear, she shouts so loud.

It's a turning, the voice comes back. What? The corridor turns left but the ship is on its side, so the left turn is actually a pit. How big is the gap, can we jump it? I can't jump, says one woman.

He hears a seagull and he thinks for a second he is up there, looking down on this. Like when his wife told him that she had been having an affair with Sean from her amateur dramatics group and they were lying there in bed and he pictured the scene; he could almost see it, like in a movie, from behind a ceiling fan, the two of them in bed, he with his eyes open saying nothing, she beside him wanting nothing more than he would say something, anything, really anything would do, but he doesn't, he didn't.

Where are you?

I'll jump, a man says, give me some room, I need a run up. He takes some steps back and he tries to run but the ceiling is too low and he can't run properly and he stops at the edge. Oh no, oh no, says another woman.

The seagull cries and he cries too. What a time to cry – what isn't a time to cry? If I can't cry before I die, when can I cry? His life has been like this, asking if he should cry and then not crying. He has never liked it when women cry; he feels like he's being tricked or coerced into feelings he doesn't really have, which he doesn't have because he asks himself if he should feel those feelings and that pushes them away. What's wrong with you?

The water lion roars. He looks back. At the end of the corridor, the water is frothing and churning.

What are we going to do? asks a man in a check shirt. I don't want to die, says a teenage girl. She says it almost to herself. At first, he frowns. Who wants to die? But does he? Does he want to die?

Clare, where are you? At home? With Sean? At a rehearsal? Re-hears-al. The word strikes him for the first time.

Driving a hearse into what is real. The driver has a skull and a top hat.

He's howling; he has real tears. He wants a child. He what?

Sir, that isn't helping anybody, says the check shirt. He looks up. Was that me?

He sees the passengers looking at him and he realises he has been crying.

I long so much to connect. I want so much to stop rehearsing for something. I want to reach out and touch.

He takes a step forward. I'll be your bridge. They don't understand him.

Help me lie down over the gap. You can use my back as a bridge.

That's not going to work, says check shirt.

Let me try. If you hold my feet on the edge and you hold my legs and ease me slowly over the gap, I'll grab onto the other side. You can walk over my back.

I'm not walking over your back.

Yes you are. Please.

And now his forearms are pressed onto the far side of the pit. There's a balled-up jacket under his shins to stop them barking on the corner. His stomach muscles are burning and grinding. He's trying not to hear the lions below.

An estate agent walks over his back. A caterer walks over his back. A garden centre manager walks over his back. An unemployed administrator and her husband in a check shirt walk over his back. A student of veterinary sciences walks over his back. A Goth who doesn't want to die walks over his back. He feels their love and their gratitude and he's not on the ceiling, he's not flying above the boat, he's not over there, he's here, he's right here, he's a bridge, he's a beautiful bridge.

In March 1987, the passenger ship Herald *of Free Enterprise left Zeebrugge with her bow doors open. The ship sank with a loss of 193 lives. A few were helped to safety by Andrew Parker, an ex-policeman, who lay across a damaged walkway and let twenty passengers walk across his back to safety. This story is an entirely imagined and fictional response to his bravery.*

BAD AT BAY

JOHN FIDLER

Yeah, you've probably seen me, mate. I stand on the high street most weekdays and every weekend, just near Holland & Barrett. It's a good spot. Gold suit and raincoat, gold shoes and socks, gold hat, gold briefcase, gold shirt and tie. And, of course, gold paint on my face and hands – any exposed bit of skin. Used to need a tin of metallic hairspray too, but I'm bald now. Probably because of the metallic hairspray.

And then I stand – absolutely stock-still but posed as if I'm running for a bus or a cab, one finger raised to flag the bugger down, tie sticking out behind me like it's being whipped back, in my slipstream sort of thing. I've got a special piece of flexible wire all along it in the lining – trade secret, that. Same inside the bottom of my raincoat, so I can make it like it's billowing out behind me. And the suitcase I hold raised up swinging back behind me – looks heavy but it isn't. Just cardboard sprayed gold, and nowt inside.

But it's all packed away in my bag now – got my civvies on. Can't sit in the pub all gold from top to bottom, can I? They'd call me Terry! Oh, look, Terry's All Gold, eh? Still got the hands and face tonight, though. Usually scrub it off in the bogs here, but I forgot my wet wipes, didn't I? Still, it's a conversation starter, innit? Got us talking, anyway.

I know what you're thinking. Money for old rope. Folk chucking gelt at him all the livelong day and him just standing there. Ha! There's hardly any dosh in it. Not any more. Not only do people have no appreciation for the performing arts, they're all faces in their phones and hustle-bustle. And the ones who aren't – pensioners mainly – save all their spare change for all these homeless they have now. I have to contend with a down-on-his-luck ex-army chap outside Santander on one side of me, and a skinny young girl with a doe-eyed Bichon Frise near Dorothy Perkins on the other.

So, no, I don't do it for the money. I'm lucky if I make enough for a couple of pints in here before I catch my bus. What's that? Oh, very kind. Pint of Boltmaker, if you don't mind.

And as for 'just' standing there, it's actually very physically demanding. You have to be very disciplined to maintain that exact pose. It's a skill. I'm actually more exhausted after a day in the pose than if I'd been scooting around the Arndale all day. Let me put it this way, I'm very grateful to the makers of Radox of an evening. So I don't do it for the good of my health, either.

I'll tell you the reason I do it.

To belong.

To have a purpose.

To save the world.

Yeah, you heard me – to save the blinking world! What from?

Demons.

Well, that's what some call 'em. Monsters, you could say, but that makes me think of that furry fella out of that kids' movie, and they're nothing like that. Not aliens, because they're not from space, they're right here with us – cheek by jowl, so to speak, but not quite. Here, but on the other side of a gossamer-thin veil. And these things, these demons, they want in.

And I'm here to stop them getting through. Me and all the others.

See, if you've travelled a bit, you'll know that you see us human statues in every big town and city, all over the world. Knights in armour. Roman soldiers. Ladies in crinolines.

Angels, giants, mermaids. A chap holding a cane who looks like he's sitting supported by thin air. All kinds – and all painted silver, gold or bronze, whatever's needed.

And all of us together, we make a kind of network that stops them breaking through, the demons. Different combinations for different days – the weather affects it, the moon, all sorts. The orders come from up the chain somewhere. And a casing of metal surrounding a human soul gives the best protection – 'the armour and the warrior within', they call it. And the poses and the conductivity of the metal help link us all together – like when you used to have to stand holding the aerial in a certain position to get the best reception on old tellies.

I'm part of something. I was alone and lonely – drifting, purposeless. Crummy job – stamping forms, filing things that nobody would ever look at. But now … now I'm part of an army, a brotherhood. By which I mean to encompass sisterhood too – siblinghood – is that a word? Anyway, I stand there on my own in the middle of town, not moving, not talking to anyone, but I'm part of a team. A brick in a wall. If I decide to walk away early, it's a little bit weaker. And all those people, rushing past me, busy with their business, ignoring me, yapping on their phones – or looking and laughing – they don't know it, but I'm keeping them … we're keeping them all safe.

Maybe they don't deserve to be saved, some of them, but they don't deserve to be gobbled up by a Gaffler either, or feel the rasp of a Skittron's tongue when they're on their way to Slimming World.

I know, I know. You're going to say it seems like the world's already being run by demons. But believe me, these things are worse. Maybe five or six times worse.

Because they have got through in the past, here and there, once in a while, before the network was put in place. Every myth you've ever read about a dragon is probably one of these.

They're not from another dimension, not quite. They're here with us. But like behind glass. We can't see them, but they're there. It's like birds banging into your window. Normally it doesn't matter – they just bounce off – but once in a while, they strike it at just the right speed and just the right angle with their beak and maybe there's a flaw in the glass and the whole window shatters into a million pieces and suddenly you've got a befuddled crow in your kitchen flapping around in your Honey Nut Loops. It happens. There's a YouTube video called 'Bird Breaks Window'. Check it out on your phone if you don't believe me. I'll wait.

See, they weren't always a big problem, the demons. When, once in a blue moon, they did accidentally get through, they might meet a St George type, or wolf down a bunch of villagers with the plague and expire in the forest a week later. But a few got through, had a few nice fat humans for dinner, and somehow slipped back through to their own side of the glass again. We think that's where the real trouble started. Word got around. How delicious we were, how plentiful, what easy prey. Where once they'd made the odd accidental incursion, now the best and brightest of the demon world were working round the clock – if they have clocks – on how to get through to the gigantic, free, fast-food buffet that is the human race. And as they slowly and surely drew their plans against us, so the secret order began to mount our defence.

Of course, I'm not supposed to talk about any of this. But in vino veritas, eh? Does that work with beer?

Am I afraid that people won't believe me, that they'll take the Michael? Listen, I stand in a high footfall area every day dressed like a giant toffee penny. So, as a great poet once said, ridicule is nothing to be scared of.

No, I'm more scared that they will believe me. Panic on the streets of Birmingham and all that. Or that the military will get wind of it – always looking for new toys, that mob. Some barmy army top brass is bound to try to bring the demons through, thinking they can tame them, harness them as weapons. What could possibly go wrong, eh?

So why am I telling you? It's no coincidence. I've had my eye on you. You're a regular in here. So am I, but I've not usually got a head like C-3PO, so you haven't noticed me. Why should you? But I've seen you. Always come in on your own. Always go out on your own. Never talk to anyone while you're here – head in a Ruth Rendell, usually. You've probably been wishing I'd leave you alone all through me talking, but you're too polite to say so. That's good – means you care about people.

And you believe me, don't you? Or you want to. I can see it in your eyes. I've got files full of evidence and history and testimonials and all sorts back at me mam's, but I just knew that I wouldn't have to bring any of it. That you'd see the truth, and you wouldn't be afraid.

Because people don't last for ever. Sometimes it's natural causes, sometimes it's supernatural causes. So we end up with chinks in the armour. Blind spots in our coverage. And they only need one. Like a mosquito finding a crack in your tent flap.

Anyway, there's a bloke down the road a ways – can't say exactly where, need to know and all that, but it's on a bus route – and he's been a silver wizard opposite the chiropodist's for thirty-odd years. Outstretched staff, floor-length cloak, pointy hat, flowing beard – false at first, but he eventually grew his own. Anyway, he's getting up there in years now, and reaching the end of his tether. His arthritis is giving him jip, his bladder's not up to the long hours any more. He wants a few years tending his rhododendrons and watching *Cash In The Attic*.

So, he's soldiering on as best he can for now, bless him, but we need a replacement sharpish. And I think you're just the fella for the job. I've watched you and you're just like I was. Adrift. Rudderless. You need a purpose. And if saving the entirety of humankind from a demonic invasion isn't a corker of a purpose, then I don't know what is. Plus you get bags of fresh air, we supply the costume and provide travel expenses – do hang on to your receipts – and you get to keep whatever shrapnel folk chuck in the hat.

What do you think? Wouldn't you like to be part of something? Wouldn't you like to belong? You'd be a hero. Unsung, but we'd know, you'd know. Think about it and let *me* know. But soon. I'm here most evenings. Or outside Holland & Barrett most days – but I can't really talk then.

OH, MY HOPELESS WANDERER

ZOE VENDITOZZI

The route she took didn't vary any more. Over the months, she'd tried almost all the streets of the village, seeking out the smoothest pavements and shortest kerbs. The only aim she had was to get the baby to sleep and to keep him asleep as long as possible. Walking for miles was infinitely preferable to being stuck in the house with the circular crying. She thanked God that Robert had been born in the spring and that she'd had the first five and a half months (not that she was counting) with relatively good weather, as she seemed to spend more time out than in.

Kate saw herself as akin to the neighbourhood cats that she saw all over the place. They were everywhere and surely knew everything that was happening, but they were largely unremarked upon and left alone. She enjoyed a similar position and that suited her fine. She'd never been particularly good with people and had hoped that joining the new mums' club might alter that in her but, if anything, she now had even less inclination to chat to people. She'd tried – really, she had – but all she thought about was feeding and walking, feeding and walking. She felt like she was doing something similar to keeping the Olympic torch lit but that she had no idea where Mount Olympus was or if she'd ever get there. Actually, wasn't the torch heading from the mountain towards the stadium? No matter, it still stood.

The pavement outside the shops was tricky to navigate because although it was one of the smoothest surfaces on the route, there were usually several people to weave around. Getting an accurate turn on the pram's wheels whilst avoiding eye contact required quite an effort of pantomiming. Kate was anticipating the usual rigmarole as she peered intently into the pram as if she was settling the baby, which was why she almost missed the teenager who was hunkered down on the ground outside the Spar. Just as she reached the huddled figure, an arm shot out, stopping the pram in its tracks. The kid, Kate couldn't tell at first if it was a boy or girl, muttered, 'Watch it!' and despite herself, Kate pulled up short and, kicking the brake on, moved to the front of the pram.

The kid was guarding something small on the pavement. As Kate edged round the kid's shoulder, she could see that a little bird was lying beak-up on the pavement.

'Oh!' she said. 'Is it OK?'

The girl, she could see now, was about fourteen and dressed in shades of black. Her fringe was so long that Kate couldn't see much of her eyes, except flashes of white. Despite this, she knew the girl was scowling and that she was always scowling and that the scowl was her keep-back, leave-me-alone face. Kate knew this because she'd made that face for a long time and had only in recent years learned to mutate it into a resting slight smile. It served the same purpose but was more befitting a grown-up woman.

However, in this instance, the care for the injured, likely dead, bird trumped the no-approach demeanour, and Kate leaned in.

'Is it breathing?'

The girl shrugged.

'Did you find it like this?'

The girl snapped her head round.

'It wasn't me!' She pushed her fringe out of her eyes. 'I didn't do anything!'

'It's OK!' Kate raised her hands. 'I'm not saying you did anything. I'm just wondering if you've seen it move at all.'

'No.' The girl sighed and crouched even lower, reaching her hand towards the bird but not touching it. 'It hasn't moved.'

Kate looked up at the shop window. 'It probably flew into that. It happens all the time.'

'I know,' the girl muttered. Clearly, she wasn't stupid. 'Do you think we should pick it up?'

'We?' Kate was not going to be touching a dead bird. The girl tutted; it seemed Kate had disappointed her. 'Maybe we should try and give it some sugar water?'

No,' the girl said, 'that's bees.'

'Oh yes, of course.'

'I'm going to pick it up.'

'Really?' Kate paused. 'I think it's …'

'Even if it's dead, I'm not leaving it here just so it can get taken by a cat or something. It's not right.'

Kate remembered the bird funerals she'd planned and officiated at as a little girl.

'Here.' She reached into the nappy bag that was under the pram and brought out a packet of tissues. 'Use one of these, at least.'

The girl nodded and reached for a tissue. Now that Kate was looking at her more clearly, she realised that she'd seen her before but usually with the group of kids that hung around in the park. She avoided them as much as possible. Not because she feared them as such, but more because they were inclined to make sudden squawks and whoops. It was too great a risk that they might waken Robert.

The girl folded the tissue out over the palm of her right hand and scooped up the bird. 'God, it doesn't weigh anything.'

Kate and the girl both stood, then leaned together, not quite touching. 'Can you feel anything? A heartbeat? Breathing?'

The girl shook her head.

'Maybe you should cup your other hand round. Warm it up a bit?'

The girl made a nest of her hands and Kate could just make out the bird's head through the space between her thumbs.

'Why are you always out walking?' The girl didn't look up at her as she spoke.

'The baby.' Kate nodded at the pram.

'I never see anyone out as much as I see you. You're always out.'

'Yep, I am.'

'Don't you have any friends?'

She knew the girl wasn't being cheeky, but Kate was mortified. 'Not here, no.'

'Are you from somewhere else?'

'Yes. But we've been here a few years.'

'We've been here for four years.'

'Really? Where are you from?'

'Poland.' Before Kate could ask her anything else, the girl spoke again. 'There's loads of women with prams.' She pronounced the o of women as if it rhymed with 'woe'. 'Why don't you just hang out with them?'

Kate shrugged. Peter sometimes asked her a variation on that question.

'Are they too stuck up?'

'No,' Kate said. 'I'm just not really looking for a friend. I like being on my own. Mostly.'

The girl nodded and looked at her again. She puffed her fringe out of her eyes through her extended lower lip.

'I get you. But you can't get away with that at my age.'

'No?'

'Nuht. People'd give me more shit than I already get for being foreign. I just hang out with folk to look normal.' She smiled, then raised her hands to her face.

'You're not going to give it mouth-to-mouth, are you?' asked Kate, not sure if she should stop her.

'No, I'm not that much of a weirdo.' The girl blew gently into her hands and then looked up sharply. 'I think it moved!'

'Really?' Kate leaned closer.

They waited. Wishful thinking, Kate thought. The girl's face fell, but then she gasped.

'It definitely moved there!'

'Open your hand a little.' Kate smiled at the girl. The girl opened her right hand as if it was on a hinge.

The bird looked just the same as they stood and studied it. Kate didn't know what it was called. A starling? A thrush? A sparrow? Something commonplace, anyway. One of those things you saw everywhere and took for granted and didn't feel the need to pin down with a name. It was mostly grey with pale brown daubs on its wings. Its face was black and its beak was broad and short. Kate took it all in – she'd need to look it up later.

As the girl stared at the bird – probably willing it into life, though there was no sign of anything – Kate looked at her hands, which were pale and freckled, with long fingers and chipped purple nails. Kate looked up at her face in profile. The girl wasn't wearing any make-up and she was pale and freckled just like her hands. She turned and looked back at Kate just as the bird twitched.

They stared, frozen, as the bird's eyes opened. They were black and shiny and it was as if the bird was merely waking from a nap. Its head turned to the left then right and with a little bunch of its muscly-seeming wee body, it flew from the girl's hand.

They stared at each other. Kate knew her expression was mirroring that of the girl's – eyes wide, mouths perfect 'o's. Then the girl laughed, seeing her hands were still held out but now empty, save for the tissue. She looked so much younger and her delight was infectious.

'Wow!' she said to Kate, staring up at where the bird had disappeared. 'Wow!'

'I know!' Kate nodded. 'That was … that was amazing …'

They stood a moment longer and the girl smiled at Kate. 'Thank you,' she said.

'I didn't do anything! You did all the holding. You brought it back to life.'

The girl blushed and smiled again. 'You stayed with me, though.'

Kate touched the girl's shoulder briefly, then took the tissue from her hand and stuck it in her pocket.

Robert snuffled in his sleep. Kate took a breath. 'I'd better go now.' She moved round the pram and nudged the brake off with her foot.

'Yeah.' The girl did a single nod. 'That pram won't walk itself.'

Kate would have liked to stay and talk to the girl, ask her name at least, but she could feel the moment getting away from them.

'See you around,' said the girl.

Kate nodded and they both set off on their separate ways.

NEARLY THERE

JOANNA CAMPBELL

Peter wanted to read his *Beano*, but it was packed away in the Things-For-The-Bus Bag. He wasn't to touch that. It stood to attention in the hall, a bulgy tartan soldier. The box of French fancies was waiting on the hall table and Peter was sitting beside it on the lino, also waiting. These things alone made today different.

They didn't normally have French fancies. And Peter wasn't supposed to sit on the floor in his good trousers – Crimplene attracted dog hair like a magnet – but Mam wasn't paying attention. Her nervy hands kept smoothing her frock even though she'd ironed it three times over instead of making dinner. Grandma had fried them a bit of liver in the end and now the house smelt of her onions, sliced into half-moons, which put Peter in mind of big toenail clippings.

Different days hung heavily. Unless it was Christmas or a birthday, and this day was neither of those. Different days usually meant illnesses or arguments. Or both. Like the time Peter was on the couch with measles, or the time Mam threw a block of vanilla ice cream at Dad.

Today was all about waiting.

Grandma, calm as you like in her navy skirt and white cardigan, which was the summer uniform for old ladies, was knitting him an orange and brown tank top in zigzag stripes that looked the same as the standard lampshade or the kitchen curtains or the tea cosy, her needles clicking through the silence. She didn't take well to upheaval either.

She had been a rebel at school, she once said. Peter didn't know why she was behaving herself now she didn't have to. No one told pensioners off. Peter's dad, on the other hand, hadn't behaved himself at all when he should be putting his dear wife and son first. He'd heard Grandma say that last year, the day his mam's face hid in her hands.

Peter stood up and went to watch out of the window. Would Dad be here in time?

Mam was worrying too.

'Will he get here by two, d'you think?' she whispered to Grandma. 'There won't be another bus after. Not all the way.'

Grandma shrugged and carried on clicking. She was stopping at home to mind the budgie and despite the excitement of the bags in the hall, Peter wished for a second he could change places with her. Dad might have changed too much. Or Mam might throw a Mr Whippy at him.

Mam was stroking Bluey's beak through the bars of the cage. She didn't normally bother with affection these days. She often looked as if she needed a hug but was too mithered to stop and ask for one. She normally just said, 'Oh, Peter, when did you last clean this cage out? Are you sure he's had a fly-around this week? Because I've not cleared up any droppings from behind the couch.'

Peter wanted to go up to Mam now she was being all fond-like and wrap his arms round her like he used to. But the crease between her eyebrows had deepened. She should have ironed that too. It made her look cross, or at least in a bit of a stew, and Peter was afraid she might push him away, so he left her alone.

'Why's the lad looking out the front window for his nibs?' Grandma asked with one of her hard sniffs to show she thought Dad oughtn't to be coming back at all, let alone through the front door. 'He'll have the sense to come round the back, won't he?'

Mam huffed out a sigh, a politer reply, Peter thought, than the words she was probably thinking.

Although his breath had steamed the glass, Peter could see a car emerging through the mist.

'He's here!'

Mam pelted into the hall and fell over the tartan bag. Peter hurdled across her and pulled the door open. A blue Mini was parked alongside the pavement. A very wide nurse heaved herself out and reached in for a large medical bag on the back seat. Peter reported this to Mam on the floor.

'Oh, that'll be the midwife for Mrs Clegg again,' she said. 'Another damned false alarm.'

This was horribly different. For days Mam had been comforting Mrs Clegg, who had gone a fortnight overdue without ever saying 'damned'. She was right vexed the one time Peter tried saying it. She'd certainly never said 'damned' while lying on the hall carpet sprawled over a tartan shopping bag. Peter wanted to help her up and he badly wanted to hug her, but then things would seem even less ordinary.

As it turned out, there was no time for wanting and thinking. Puffed out and red-faced, the midwife lumbered up their path and begged for Mam's help to grip hold of Mrs Clegg's bedstead. The baby was coming fast, she couldn't stop shaking and the bed was skittering about the bedroom floor. Peter was needed to look after little Jimmy Clegg, who couldn't understand the sudden fuss and refused to be confined to the front room.

Mam dashed off, her starched petticoat rustling, the midwife's uniform crackling.

Peter hesitated for a second. Although he knew better, he wanted to take his *Beano* out of the tartan bag and a pink fancy from the box, and give them to Jimmy. Maybe you could be forgiven for a small wrongdoing if it was for a good reason. He hoped this was one of those times.

It was strange being next door, in a mirror reflection of his own house. Everything much the same, but different, the rooms set out the other way round. He read the comic to Jimmy and explained the pictures, in between picking up crumbs and trying to drown out the sounds from upstairs by making Dennis the Menace repeat himself at full volume.

While Mrs Clegg was still labouring upstairs and Mam was gripping on for dear life, Peter heard a car rumble to a standstill.

If he rushed outside, Jimmy would follow. And he'd been told to keep him in. It was important to obey instructions because Grandma said Dad was hopeless at doing as he was told and if Peter wasn't careful, people would say 'like father, like son'. The smallest misdeed would set their tongues wagging.

He picked Jimmy up, great lump though he was and sticky all over with cake crumbs, and opened the front door. But he didn't cross the threshold. Not even one toe touched the step. But he wanted to, wanted it with more urgency, he was sure, than even Mrs Clegg was suffering in her hour of need.

Because climbing out of a taxi into the pouring rain was Dad.

Not like dads normally do, with their grey raincoats over one arm and their cigarettes hanging from the edge of their smiles. Peter's dad looked a bit shy and also confused at his own door being closed while his son looked on from Mrs Clegg's.

He didn't know about the surprise holiday that would take him away from the friends who might tempt him straight back into trouble. He didn't know Peter and Mam were helping Mrs Clegg. He probably did know that Grandma was knitting in her chair, in no hurry to invite him in.

Peter ached inside, a clawing feeling that had nothing to do with Jimmy's feet kicking his stomach. He'd missed his dad, missed him without knowing how badly until now.

The rain pounding on his hat, Dad walked across to Peter, slow-like, as if he wasn't sure if he was welcome. He still smelt of coal-tar soap and peppermints. He said hello in the voice Peter remembered even after a whole year. And when Peter said hello back, Dad spread his arms wide.

Then a baby started bawling and Mam came rushing down the stairs, straight into Dad's arms. Peter, still grappling with Jimmy, all smeared with pink icing and struggling in his arms, watched the 97 bus hiss through puddles, the brakes wheezing to a standstill outside the house.

Mam let go of Dad and picked up his case. She didn't need to say anything to Peter. He charged back inside with Jimmy and took him up to meet his new brother. Then he ran home, gathered the bags and dragged them into the bus. There was no time to go back for the fancies, Dad's treat for the journey. Any minute now, after twitching the net curtain back into place, Grandma would be wolfing them down. The thought of that made them seem a bit less fancy.

Mam tugged Dad's sleeve. 'Come on, my love,' she said.

He followed like an obedient child and they climbed on just as the conductor dinged the bell, squashing together on the seat beside Peter. The bus reeked of damp clothes and the steaming nylon of soaked umbrellas, a proper holiday smell.

'We're off, then,' Mam said.

It was something Dad used to say every summer. And he also said, 'Wave goodbye to the house!' And the best one, once they were ten miles from the guest house, 'Can you smell the sea?'

Peter hoped he would say it today. It wouldn't be right if Mam did all the talking. Dad unfolded his handkerchief and wiped a clear path through the misted window. Perhaps he was trying to work out where they were going, but they only ever went to Mablethorpe. Some things never changed. Dad should know that.

'A great big boy he is,' Mam was saying about the Clegg baby. 'Not as bonny as our Peter was, though.'

The crease between her eyes was fainter. Maybe the brand-new Clegg had unstiffened it. Babies made ladies go a bit soft.

'Came out like a rocket in the end,' she said. 'Thank heaven, else we'd have missed the bus. I never even had a moment to say goodbye to Grandma.'

'She'll keep,' Dad said.

'Aye, some things always stay the same.'

'Nowt wrong with that.'

It seemed to Peter that Dad forgave Grandma for disapproving of him more easily than she forgave him for his misdeeds. And Mam didn't even need to forgive Dad, because she was so glad to see him. All her upset had long ago melted with the ice cream on the hearthrug.

They were smiling right in each other's faces, like they used to in the days before Mam was vexed with him. Peter hoped Dad wouldn't say he was turning over a new leaf, because he'd said that before and no leaves were ever turned. Or if they were, they soon dropped off and drifted away in the wind. That was why, at the merest mention of him, Grandma had to be forgiven for screwing up her lips as if she'd swallowed a wasp. She was tired of leaves crisping and rusting and skating along the ground.

Mam gave Dad the cigarettes she had bought for him and he kept on smiling, but he couldn't hold it there, as if his face muscles were working the wrong way round. And Peter saw it, the tear sliding down. And, like she'd chanced upon a drop of water after years of being stranded in the desert, Mam kissed the tear.

This wasn't at all normal. Peter had to look away from such a private thing. It felt like wandering into a birthday party without an invitation. Or going into the Cleggs' with everything familiar but reshuffled. Jimmy must have felt the same, but the other way about; still in his own home, but with different people there and his mam's carpet sweeper lying on the floor where she'd abandoned it.

As the town clattered by and the countryside stepped in, the strange day began to settle into something like normal. It was probably calming down at the Cleggs' too, as the crying baby took its place in the routine. Mrs Clegg was probably out of bed and making the tea, picking up her carpet sweeper where she'd left it and wondering why there were so many crumbs.

When Peter tired of watching raindrop-crawling races, he looked up to see Mam resting her head on Dad's shoulder the way she used to when they listened to the wireless in the evenings, and Dad eating the teatime sandwiches from the tartan bag even though he wasn't meant to until they were on the beach. All of that was ordinary enough.

In a voice that was a bit quieter and shakier than Peter remembered, Dad said, 'There it is. Can you smell it, son?'

Peter breathed in hard and, even though there was not the smallest trace of a salty tang in the stuffy bus, he said, 'Yes. Yes, I can, Dad. Are we nearly there?'

And Dad and Mam both said, 'Yes, son. We nearly are.'

SINGING IN THE DARK TIMES

PAULINE MELVILLE

It was a fine summer morning in June. Office workers streamed in and out of Finsbury Park tube station. Most people kept their heads down except for the tramp standing just outside the entrance. He was squinting up at the blue sky. He attracted attention because he was the only person who looked strikingly alive – albeit destitute. There was a burning vigour in his red cheeks that might have derived from sheer exposure to open-air living, or from methylated spirits. Compared to the commuters, whose features seemed to have been modelled in soft wax, blurring any distinction between them, he stood out like a Rembrandt portrait – all warts and whelks, with a face that had been forged in adversity and realised by a master painter. He had a bushy head of grey hair, a broad nose threaded with a network of purple veins and he wore a greasy greatcoat – old army issue with umpteen pockets – that was tied around the waist with string. His eyes were bright blue but without lashes. Two strands of beads were visible under the collar of his coat.

Having finished examining the sky, he fumbled for an old leather shoe with the sole flapping off. This he held to his right ear and spoke into as if it were a mobile phone:

'Hello. I'm in Finsbury Park. Where are you?' With his left

hand he motioned passers-by impatiently towards the cap on the ground, which had a few coins in it.

After a while, tired of this one-way conversation, he wandered over to a nearby parking meter to feel in the metal cavity for any forgotten coins. Returning to his post, he interrupted the flow of people to ask a man in black-rimmed spectacles for some change. The man swerved and hurried on.

'Piss off then, you four-eyed twat,' the vagrant called after him cheerily.

From spring onwards, with the rising of the sap, all manner of tramps sprout up alongside the daffodils and by the summer they are bedding down in parks and doorways all over town. In the hierarchy of vagrants, Hoagy B., as he was known, considered himself to be somewhere near the top.

'I am a Tippel-Brother,' he would announce, should anyone ask. It was while stationed in Germany that he had come across the *Tippelbrüder*. They were known as 'orderly wanderers'. Their way of life appealed to him and he made a note of it for when he was demobbed. Apparently, in the glory days there had been an International Brotherhood of Vagrants in Germany. To cap it all, Hamburg had even hosted a Vagrants' Congress attended by 300 of them. Rot set in when a vagrants' registration was introduced.

Hoagy B.'s main occupation was walking. For more years than he could remember, he had spent his time trudging from John O'Groats to Land's End and back again. He would go from farm to farm, getting fed for a day's work cutting grass, house painting, picking fruit, sometimes staying for up to a week and then heading off once more. When he needed money, he would venture into the nearest town and find casual work as a navvy, wielding a pickaxe or pneumatic drill on the roads for a while. But there was no work to be found in London this year and he had been reduced to a little light begging – not his preferred style.

He looked down at his watch and started back with a theatrical gesture as though the watch had affronted him in some way.

'Is that the time already?' he muttered.

This was all the more extraordinary because he had no watch. There was nothing on his wrist except a few pieces of string plaited together. Next to where he stood, his old brown nylon sleeping bag lay sodden after the night's rainstorm. As he held it up to inspect it, the sleeping bag came apart in his hands. He kicked it into a doorway. Then he collected his cap, put the few coins in his pocket and set off.

A short while later he was seen striking out towards Hyde Park, now with an empty milk bottle to his ear, chatting in tandem with other members of the public who were also glued to their phones.

'Hang on. I can't roll a fag while I've got a telephone in my hand,' he said, and stopped to throw the bottle in a litter bin before taking out his tobacco tin and continuing on his way.

Just before he entered the park something caught his eye. In a skip next to some iron railings was an old-fashioned defunct Ferguson twelve-inch television. Hoagy fished it out and tucked it under his arm.

That June day the park was dotted with idlers in deckchairs, couples smooching on the grass and clerical workers tucking into their lunch-break sandwiches. Looking for a more secluded spot, Hoagy walked through Hyde Park and on to Kensington Gardens. There he took up residence on an empty park bench sheltered by trees near the statue of Peter Pan. He put the television down on the ground and sat down. From one of his pockets he pulled out a sock. In it were some hard-boiled eggs. Then he rummaged until he found two other small packets containing salt and pepper. After he had finished eating, he cocked his legs up on the bench, put his arms behind his head and gazed at the television.

A man shot by on a bicycle, his wispy white hair flying from under an orange baseball cap. He sat upright and whistled as he went. On his back he carried what looked like a canvas quiver with multi-coloured plastic windmills poking out from the top. When he spotted the tramp and the television, he put his feet on the ground and skidded to a halt, then pushed himself backwards towards Hoagy.

'Anything good on?' He was well spoken with a lightweight, amused and slightly coquettish manner.

'Not much,' Hoagy replied. 'There's always something missing when you're watching television, isn't there? It's the woman coming round with ice creams.' The man rested his bicycle against a tree and joined Hoagy, who shifted along the bench:

'I'm taking these windmills to the children of Grenfell. They will want toys as well as blankets. Something beautiful, eh? Bread and roses. We all have to do whatever we can. There's a collection centre in Walmer Road. Although I hear that they already have too much stuff.'

'What's happened at Grendel?' Hoagy enquired in a voice that retained traces of a Welsh accent.

'No. Grenfell. Grendel's a different monster altogether.' The man threw back his head and laughed. 'Beowulf defeated Grendel. But the dragon hoarding the treasure was the one who did for Beowulf in the end. Kensington Borough Council in this case. Have you not heard about it? The tragedy? It was three days ago.'

'Can't say I have, professor,' said Hoagy. He nodded towards the television. 'It weren't on the news.'

'Grenfell Tower went up in flames.' All the laughter fell away from the man, who suddenly looked distraught. There was silence between the two for several minutes. A hard-boiled egg was pulled out from the sock and offered to the stranger, who declined it with a shake of his head. Hoagy stood up and took a shining tin can from one of his pockets. He walked slowly over to the small lake opposite and helped himself to a drink of water.

Then, to the elderly cyclist's astonishment, Hoagy turned to face him and began to sing, his chest expanding under the old army coat. Even more surprising, out of his mouth came a melodious and tuneful tenor voice:

> You've heard of the Gresford disaster
> And the terrible price that was paid,
> Two hundred and forty-two colliers were lost
> And three men of the rescue brigade.
> Now the Lord Mayor of London's collecting
> To help out the children and wives.
> The owners have sent some white lilies, dear God,
> To pay for the poor colliers' lives.

'Yes,' said the cyclist, the twinkle now back in his eye. 'You're right to sing. How does that quotation go? "In the dark times will there also be singing? Yes, there will also be singing – about the dark times." Is that a trained tenor voice I detect?'

'Yes. Once. Before the army. A while back,' Hoagy growled. He frowned and spat on the ground.

The cyclist put on his cap and bent to adjust his cycle clips.

At that point a ladybird flew on to the frayed cuff of Hoagy's coat, folding its wings back under the scarlet-and-black-dotted shell. He tried without success to shake it off. The man mounted his bicycle.

'I'll be on my way. Good luck.'

'And to you, sir.' Hoagy watched him cycle off. 'Fly away home,' he said to the ladybird.

Several hours later Hoagy B. found himself standing in Walmer Road. He looked up to see, a few blocks away, the towering, blackened ruin. Shocked at the sight, he backed into a doorway and rolled himself a cigarette. The street was noisy and crowded. People of all sizes and descriptions shouted encouragement to each other, pushing trolleys of bottled water and struggling with plastic bags full of clothes, while others manhandled crates of soft drinks. Trestle tables had been set up, piled with a variety of foods and fruits and yet more water bottles. Cars were parked skew-whiff in the road with their boots open as people ferried goods to various destinations.

The doors of the Westway Centre were wide open. Hoagy approached and peeped inside. Close to the doors were rows of charcoal-grey sports mats and foam mattresses laid out in formal lines. Some contained sleeping figures. On others sat small family groups. There was a hum of organised activity. A short, dark-haired woman stood on a chair directing proceedings, ordering a chain of helpers who were passing armfuls of bedding, blankets and sleeping bags to each other. The woman shouted instructions: 'This bedding is surplus. Put it in a pile near the door. A van will collect the surplus and take it for storage in a warehouse. The table at the back is for toiletries, nappies, etcetera.' She gesticulated to show where everything should go, while volunteers milled about helping wherever they could.

Two yards from Hoagy, a small boy of about nine with a cinnamon complexion and shining black eyes stood holding his grandfather's hand. The man wore a white calf-length tunic and red soft-soled slippers. He was in his fifties with a small white beard, a long nose and eyes as black, though not as brilliant, as his grandson's. He squatted down and spoke to a plump woman wearing a red salwar kameez, who was seated on a mat behind him. The man said something to the boy in a language Hoagy did not understand. Then the boy spoke to one of the volunteers who was squeezing sleeping bags into their nylon holders and tossing them to one side: 'My mum says where's the bathroom.'

The volunteer explained and the boy went and translated the answer to his mother, who heaved herself up from the floor and made her way in the direction pointed out to her.

Hoagy edged towards the pile of sleeping bags.

'Are any of these going?' he enquired.

The young woman flicked back her fair hair and looked at the tramp with suspicion.

'Are you a Grenfell victim?

'No.'

'Well, I'm really sorry, but all this had been donated for Grenfell victims only. Sorry.' She went over to alert her colleagues to the unwanted arrival of a tramp. The little boy stood staring at Hoagy. The grandfather stroked his beard and asked his grandson what was going on. He bent his ear to listen then raised his eyebrows and lifted his palms upward in a gesture of helplessness.

A solid, middle-aged black woman in a brightly patterned dress bore down on Hoagy. Full of righteous indignation she confronted him: 'Out. Out. Out. Please. We don't want freeloaders. People have lost everything here. We're all pulling together. The whole community is trying. You should be helping. Not scrounging. Go away, please.'

Hoagy hesitated, then pointed at the sleeping bags. 'I heard they were spare.'

At that point a balding council official, who had been advised to remove his identity badge because of local hostility, stepped smoothly forward.

'I'll deal with this.'

He gripped Hoagy by the arm and propelled him into the street.

'Isn't it funny,' Hoagy said as he was pushed out of the door, 'that all we derelicts have wonderful heads of hair and all you officials and bankers are bald. When did you last see a bald tramp?' Having nearly tripped as he was ejected, he stood outside on the road for a few moments to gather himself. It was early evening. The bustle in the street had subsided. Here and there people stood around in subdued groups talking in lowered voices. A few blocks away the setting sun shone through the charred tower block, turning it a rusty reddish colour as if its DNA contained a memory of fire.

Hoagy started to walk away. He had gone fifty paces when there was a tug on his sleeve. He looked down. The boy with the lustrous black eyes was standing there his arms barely able to hold the sleeping bag and the bedroll. Hoagy accepted them. The boy gave a skip and scampered off towards where the grandfather stood just outside the doors, watching out for the boy. Hoagy lifted his right arm to touch the side of his bushy hair in a sort of salute.

By the time Hoagy reached Latimer Road station, it was dark. The train on the elevated track rattled and shook its way through the buildings. Each carriage was illuminated. Hoagy watched the train pass, showing scenes of daily life: in one compartment a man read a newspaper; in another, a woman leaned across to wipe her child's face. Hoagy turned his head to one side and twisted it. That was how Grenfell Tower used to be, each flat, like one of the compartments, containing a scene of everyday life. The train was like a vertical section of Grenfell travelling on its side instead of going upwards.

He staked his pitch outside Latimer Road tube station. The station was closed. He sat on the pavement and unpacked the sleeping bag. It was brand new. He undid the leather straps of the bedroll and unfolded it to have a look before tying it up again. Then he leaned back against the wall of the station. The last train rumbled past. After a while he put the bedding down and stood up to shake his head and stretch his arms. He took some deep breaths and hummed a little, as if trying to find the right key.

By nightfall most of the inhabitants of the Westway Centre had been found hotel accommodation. There were a few left to sleep as best they could on the mattresses provided. None of those who remained recognised what they were hearing, but it penetrated the dreams of some and even those half asleep were soothed by it. One woman sat up to listen, entranced. From somewhere not too far away came the sound, floating on the night air, of a beautiful tenor voice singing one part of the duet from Bizet's *The Pearl Fishers*. The song was repeated several times and then stopped.

The next morning Hoagy made an early start and headed west towards Ealing, and away from London.

THE FREE SKATER

SUSAN E. BARSBY

3.30 a.m. and no one about. The illuminated Council House dome reached into the black above, the light combining with the moon to reveal his goal.

He put the bag down and stood staring, his pounding heart ruining the silence. A deep breath, a little shake, and he opened the rucksack to get his skates out. They had a pleasing weight in his hand; the lacing familiar, the leather and inner soles felt like part of his feet.

His blade sliced through the black nylon netting like a hot knife through butter and he hauled himself onto the barrier.

One skate got caught. One leg sliding beneath him as he wobbled and twisted, trying to work the end out. Finally, freedom. He looked across the ice.

It was perfect. There was a glow to it, an otherworldly sheen with streaks of silver, mauve, pearl. Their machine had smoothed the surface. Daytime marks had been swept away and it was fresh and new again. He looked at the stars, the moon, the twinkling tree lights, the market cabins with their topping of fake snow. It made him catch his breath.

The city was silent. The city was asleep.

His first stroke screeched and echoed around the silent buildings. He stuttered to a halt, heart banging again as he looked over his shoulder, expecting to see people running. Nothing. He tried again. Nervous strides to start with, but then he remembered his lessons.

The first lesson had been the worst, obviously. The whispering doubts in his head were screaming at him then. Approaching the rink full of teenagers and a couple of young mums, all of them staring at him. *What is he doing here?* Did he dare, would it work, could he do it? Better to stay at home and carry on with the old routine. Just put up with the noise and the bother; you're past it, old man.

He had a story of wanting to take the grandchildren, worried they'd see right through it and him. But he was welcomed. The first time he fell it shook his bones to the core. Oh, he felt his age then, wet jeans and red in the face. They all fell that day. Somehow he got used to it and found the best way to pick himself up. The teens stopped joking, the mums said hello; they accepted him.

The noise had always been with him. From his father's shouts and slaps to the school playground and then on to the factory floor, the football terraces, and at home with Alice chattering, the children playing, the Sunday routine of the lawnmower and the low rumble of the pub. It went on and on. It hadn't bothered him as a kid, but as he grew older he wanted to escape. Now tinnitus and traffic added to the mix. Supermarkets, TV, bother, voices, loud, loud, loud.

He didn't tell anyone what he really wanted to do. It remained a secret, a nugget he could retreat to when the noise all got too much. A fluke how he'd thought of it, a diverted bus route home, a glimpse of people gliding across the frozen water, a vision of freedom and of peace. And now here he was.

The ice seemed to expand as he moved. He zoomed round the rink, faster and faster, unaware of anything apart from the sound of his skates cutting through the silence and the feel of the cold night air against his face. The constant roar in his head – traffic, machinery, tinnitus, chatter – all of it finally quiet.

He'd done it. He was here – skating, whirling, floating across the ice. Just him.

Everything else had faded away.

Cleaners and barmen on their way through the square paused to watch him move with grace and poise around the ice. The CCTV cameras silently recorded his progress. A media-savvy operator would post the footage on social media tomorrow, but for now he had a limited audience.

He skated for an hour, climbed back over the barrier and through the net. After removing his skates and placing them back in his rucksack, he pulled out a length of string and repaired the hole he'd made. Job done, he picked up his bag and walked back to the taxi rank. The smile didn't leave his face till he was back next to Alice, asleep as soon as his head hit the pillow.

The skating marks on the ice glistened in the morning sun. The city woke and its people carried on with their daily routine.

AM SONTAG

A. L. KENNEDY

She must have been tired, because she kept on sleeping long after the daylight had happened.

Nobody came. Nobody woke her.

The sunheat must have lolled across the golden floorboards without her, longer and longer, like a stretching dog. The birds must have sung without her. They were singing now. That fly against one of the windows, trying to drive itself out through the glass; it must have already been failing without her. All of the world had gone on without her.

And the fly is failing still. Left window, right window – the small beating of its pointless will is audible while it goes nowhere, again and again. Here she is, watching, and there it is, failing. Anything else would violate the rule that governs nature: *given time, everything fails*.

She has come alert all of a piece – noticing, noticing, wary – and with one quickly indrawn breath. This is her habit: to surface as if from drowning, or some other suffocation. It is also her habit to arrange an inward pour of details, to be greedy for any trace of risks. For a long time now she has kept some hard thing wedged into the meat of her awareness. It therefore remains open, no matter what. The hard thing is not curiosity. It may be fear. She certainly feels she is the opposite of brave, is always an urgent animal left alone on a blank, wide meadow – perspectives, perspectives, perspectives – her skin a concealment for helpless and racing blood.

This new tall room is gentle, though. It holds only the light from two windows, the fly, the heat, one chair, this bed. None of this is trying to kill her, although each object could be adapted for killing. This would be natural.

By the far wall, there is an empty clothes rail with wheeled feet and thumbscrew adjustments for height. That looks medical and she can't like it, even though it may be meant to help her.

What good use could it have? She no longer has clothes beyond what she wore to get here – the clothes you stand up in – and none of them are hers. That stuff is folded on and over the solitary chair – this bentwood type of thing you might see in a café. As if there are surviving cafés, or have ever been cafés. People sitting outside on bentwood chairs in the warm of a Sunday afternoon and eating and drinking and smiling under the unconcealing open air …

The chair is all patterns: simple, braced curves that add up to an obvious and reckless beauty.

If you're sensible, you will stay away from beauty.

By existing it demands its own destruction. In people it is unforgivable.

She is lying inside the strangeness of a strange place and – out in out – letting her lungs fill with somewhere hardly even glimpsed when she arrived last night.

After midnight.

Stumbling along in those abrasive little hours that always stink of dying, she had been consumed, even protected, by the weird effort of undressing and washing. She had accepted exhaustion and it had blurred every surge of emotion. Her memory of most yesterdays is in slivers and this is good.

She is used to strange places, but this one is trying to bribe her so that she'll like it, offering gifts.

They sometimes do that.

And the clothes rail still worries her – it will be unkind later. A person might come, people might come, people will come and pick up the empty wire coat hangers and use them …

None of what's here is for her. She is not a person and can't need it. Is this a joke?

There are sometimes jokes. Laughing is popular, improvising – tools and implements and anything to hand, or little favourite toys – you can see the delight they add – that and the practised effort, ease.

Or is everything here in spite of her, and none of her business? That's a better thought.

She looks at her clothes, which are not her clothes but only a series of accidents. They are terrible and should be burned. What they must have brought with them ought to be destroyed.

They look guilty.

And they have the smell on them, the stink. The idea of stinking is in them for ever the way that it is in her.

Her breathing rises, rises and the bed sways like a foundering boat.

She makes herself still in the way any animal might in a field – holds on to the edges of the mattress and does nothing that would draw any predator's eye. She knows how to be unremarkable and unchallenging and still.

Nothing has happened yet and she has rested. She has the benefit of that.

She tries and can't remember solitude. This could be waiting.

She moves on to her right side – there is a ripple of aches and tenderness when she does – her attention drawn by light pealing down from those two high, unbroken windows. The floor at their foot shines with some variety of old contentment and is not pitted and has no footprints. Dust flecks turn and glint.

Nothing has been harmed.

When she swallows she can taste air that has the flavours of a long peace. It is stupid and slow. Above her the unblemished ceiling is white, ornamented with plaster shapes. It is brave. A single dark trail of old cobweb wags in some unnoticeable breeze. This demonstrates that insignificant things can be thrown about with immense ease.

On the white walls there is a small mark *there*.

And *here*.

I shall report the marks if I have to.

No, I shan't say.

I will blame the children, if there are children.

No, I will never blame children.

I will hope they go unnoticed.

I will hope the marks go unnoticed.

They may be a trap. The marks. The children.

Traps are popular.

But this doesn't taste like a trap.

Other than the cobweb, the place is neat. There is no blood. She waits for a brief sweat to ease.

I am my own fault. But peace for now. No, I am their fault. Peace and neatness.

I am somewhere neat.

I am somewhere that is beautiful.

She feels this may be everything that she has ever wanted – peace, neatness – but it has arrived at a time when she cannot believe it. People with a bag believe things.

Why keep pictures you can't look at?

When you have a bag, painkillers, papers, money, an ornament from a mantelpiece, jewellery, pictures, a toy, pullovers, milk – the idiot muddle of things you have chosen to carry.

Peace and neatness.

Your bag shows you are a person and a person can believe.

Inside my skin I am somewhere filthy.

She cannot remember when she lost her bag.

Iamfilthyfuckingdigustingwhorefilth.

In her shoe – *stupidstupidwhorebitch* – she'd hidden extra money. Its rubbing had made a sore place. Her wealth had made it more difficult to walk and you always have to.

But now there is peace and neatness.

Being able to walk is more important than food, water, money, pictures, anything.

If you possess possessions, you won't avoid the loss, you will increase it. You will have more to take away. Begin with nothing, because no one can take that.

Inside her skin there is something smeared on her bones like grease and it stinks.

No.

I have nothing and so I can keep the peace and neatness.

She tries to persuade her breathing that this is true.

Just the peace.

She tries only to like a little, gently, only to notice quietly, the blue-painted table beside the bed and, on the table, is a blue tin clock. They match. They look nice.

At some point you get taught how to make things match and look nice and you keep on with it so that you will be …

The clock ticks gently like a metal hen feeding in an endless abundance.

Then you stop.

The table might only just have been painted, finished while

she slept, it is so flawless. Her gaze passes over it and she realises that she's hoping, increasingly anxious, to find even a small chip, scratch, indication that it is not perfect. She thinks she had better not touch it.

The clock says it is one thirty and the daylight says it is the afternoon.

So much sleep and all of it just for me.

She cannot avoid making a shape with her mouth that is like smiling.

Still in peace. So much you can hear a clock tick.

They'd left her be. They had perhaps forgotten she was here. Oh, but she is, though.

She risks moving her arms a little and feels them smoothing between layers of infinitely soft cloth. This niceness, solitude, sunlight – it's like an expression of kindness, the sort of innocence that gets adjusted

It's hard to imagine how she arrived, or that she truly has done. There have been dreams before of getting out and lying in a clean bed, specifically a soft clean bed.

The clock ticks and sounds as if it isn't counting down the time to anything.

She cannot recall dreaming of floorboards and high windows. She is in a bed, then, maybe. A proper bed. A quiet bed.

A bed with nothing wrong.

A chill moves over her face, her back.

No. Peace. Kind, nice peace. A kind nice bed.

White sheet, white quilt, white pillows.

And soft.

It all feels like hiding and like being much younger and a good girl and put to bed so that she will be better after some trivial illness, or simply just safe, safe, safe at the end of a too-long day.

You tuck them in, you kiss their forehead, you say what you always say even though they are asleep already, because their body will hear and will remember. You do your best. You do.

She presses the quilt to her face and breathes in the scent of a laundry soap which is unfamiliar, but also clearly of the family of laundry soaps. She likes that it is unfamiliar. She swallows and she closes her eyes and the room drops for seconds, or for minutes, or forever, drops like dead weight that has been overtaken by dark water.

And then there's this sound.

Tang, tang, tang, tang.

It's not a bad sound.

And, yes, what first woke her, she realises – **tang, tang** – was this repeating and musical sound.

Tang, tang.

And she knows it and it isn't a sign of anything going wrong.

It is, it is, it is an expression of tranquillity.

I am a person who knows these words and I have been able to think them easily and write them and I have said them. There were times with furniture and clocks and quiet voices.

At the beginning, we still had our ideas.

I did not learn the new ideas fast enough.

I think we were philosophical. I think we called it that.

Tang. Tang.

The notes are sweet in the way that blossom is sweet, white blossom in clots, or the way that fingers close around your finger and say something which does not involve words.

We called ourselves a number of things.

The notes repeat and go climbing from low to high but only gently, four tries on one level note, four on the next.

That is what a piano sounds like.

Tang, tang. Tang, tang.

So this must be a piano.

I will call it that.

There are many rules in the world and it is impossible to know all of them. But there is a piano and pianos are not part of the rules.

Hope is a child's thing and she isn't a child.

But there is a piano.

The notes – **tang, tang** – do not provoke anything. And when she turns where she lies, there is a little rawness, but there is still no sign of the mud, which is no longer the colour of mud because too many things have happened and sunk into it. She breathes and tries not to sound like a dog running.

The soft pops of pianosound are slipping like fish, birds, fluttering like cloth, like cloth which is caught by wires, by branches, by cold things, but still moving.

There is a piano.

And the sunlight on the golden floor is beautiful and the pale shine of cleanliness is beautiful and the regular peck of the clock is beautiful and the fly is still fighting the windows and the thought of it not winning and not understanding that it never will tears her in a place under her ribs.

Tang.

She looks at the stupidly confident chair and then she is standing.

Huge room.

She is perhaps tiny.

Big house. Must be. Grandeur.

She has become nervous of large buildings because of what they could contain.

But there's a piano. Big house. Big home. Ornamentation.

How anyone could have the right to so much of all this – the idea defeats her. She would like to be furious. This swings once or twice in her skull, but steadies.

And now she's walking fast, but silent – always be silent – on stiff legs, weakish legs. She checks that no one has taken her shoes, the ones she got somewhere and which are too big but waterproof. She mumbles her fingers over the sleeves of a shirt, other things, the tired cloth. The stink lifts and shoves up at her.

She would like to scream.

Inside the coat pocket is a stone. It has no significance; it is just a stone from somewhere else, which she has brought here. She has the power to bring something from one place to another.

I don't have a religion. I have the stone.

She waits, balanced above the threat of looking down at herself and seeing what she is now. She risks looking back at the bed instead and it is disarranged as if a person has slept in it, but there is no stain. There is no purple black terrible proof of the anything.

And she can wash again. There is a bathroom.

Last night made me cry.

She walks over towards its door, which is half open but probably safe, certainly safe, and peers in.

See? It's fine.

There is only the usual – this is usual – shower stall, toilet, sink.

Tang, tang, tang, tang.

There are washing things in tiny bottles and a stack of clean, clean, harmless towels. Toothbrush in a pack, just the way you might buy it from a shop.

Toothpaste in a doll-sized tube, which reminds her of the

way she will always hate dolls for having senseless eyes and not breathing.

There is a mirror to avoid.

She plays at brushing her teeth the way that reasonable people with a future do and is mostly unaware that she is crying again. Violent peppermint is happening in her mouth.

She spits and tastes the stink and spits again and does this over and over until she retches.

Tang, tang, tang, tang.

But there is a piano.

And she uses the shower again for a long while and washes and washes and scrubs. She performs a variety of actions which animals have never mastered. She weeps in the way animals do not.

And, in the end, she does look down at her feet, ankles, legs, at herself. She is much older than before. She is different.

But I appear to be clean. I would look that way.

There is no shouting and no blood.

I do not want anyone ever to look and no one will.

Tang, tang, tang, tang.

She wraps herself in a towel and knows, for an instant, this has happened a hundred, a hundred times before.

Weakness nuzzles against the damp on her arms, her neck; she can't say its name. She wants to do damage. She pictures herself picking up the blue clock and smashing it against a wall, throwing it through a window. It would be impossible to forgive this.

But there is a piano.

And someone is playing the piano.

No. Ridiculous.

No, someone is tuning, yes, tuning, someone is tuning a piano.

So many things are necessary for this to happen, so much civility between strangers.

For an instant she is afraid but then the laughing begins. It drags at her chest and keeps on and becomes a new word for exhaustion and a type of complaint and then just a yowl.

She hears herself make noises which are not unfamiliar. They are like her clothes; they have been used before by other people.

The tears creep down her cheeks and feel like flies crawling on her face and it takes a while for them to stop.

Then she gets dressed.

Tang, tang, tang, tang.

The piano means she can bear to go and stand by the windows and see a lawn which gently sinks towards a silk expanse of water. There are the ghosts of invaded flower beds and thick explosions of unpermitted life.

There is a visible far shore, riverbank, lakeside, which is clothed in woods. Near the raw edge of the lawn there are the heads of people who are alive. The upwards burst of their shoulders and torsos when they stand is not distressed. They are shrouded in sun spatters and glints, have brown and easy limbs. They swim.

She does not want them to die, but she cannot stay inside the room while they are there.

But there is a piano.

It is frightening to listen and listening at the other available door, which is not locked and which leads into a long, lean passageway. Here there are closed white-painted doors and more white-painted walls. Nothing goes wrong.

She reaches stairs and they give her proof that she is on the uppermost floor of wherever this is. A complicated and ugly little vault rests above her and here is a plummet below, stone steps winding round it, keeping it in.

She could jump now and be finished but some ache, a softness against her spine, prevents it. So she walks downwards instead.

No.

The next floor offers a girl child and another passage. There is a child, a child, a child, a child and more doors and there is this girl child sitting.

No.

Hunch-shouldered in a green dress and bare feet, there is this girl.

There is a piano.

The girl is alone. When she lifts her face she has eyes with a broken stare, these dull lamps of emptiness.

I am the same. I have beast eyes.

The girl loses interest and drops her gaze back to the naked floorboards between her outstretched legs, begins running fingers along the spaces between the boards.

A far door opens and a thin man steps out as if he is pushing himself through water. He says something, which is probably in a language. When he realises someone unexpected has arrived his hands lift and make the shapes of being innocent and being not there. He approaches, wary and apologetic, and then halts before he is too close and sits down in clockwork stages beside the girl. The child ignores him. He seems to find this troubling.

Perhaps because of the girl's fingers, or emotion, or tiredness, the lines between the boards appear to gather speed in some manner and they push and it is possible to leave the child and the man to find that there are more steps, another flight of stairs that sinks away and leads to the first floor.

No one.

An absence of people is usually what she seeks but it is lacerating now she has turned away from these strangers and her heart believes they were her oldest friends and that they have passed through the worst together and that she should turn round again and go back. Except they were no one she knew and this seems like a betrayal by a building which is so full of peace and has a piano and should be entirely generous.

The passage leads to a final curve of more confident, wider steps, which drop down into a broad, high hallway and clearly intend to expose whoever walks on them. Still, she continues, being careful. It is quite likely that she would have the strength to run if necessary.

At this lowest level there is a kitchen noise and the smell of vegetables and a meat of some variety. These are the scents of preparing a meal for later in a place that makes sense and has an idea of later. If there is a piano and food then perhaps she may be able to eat and perhaps eating will not be shameful, although it prolongs life. Hunger swipes through her and she steadies one hand against the wall.

Tang, tang, tang, tang.

And she permits the piano to call her, passes into the emptiness of the hallway with its views into a room with odd tables, arm chairs, sitting figures she won't examine for fear of becoming visible – when you look, they feel you looking – or for fear of being mistaken, for fear of needing to recognise a face, the lie of a back, the rhythm of steps.

Somewhere a voice murmurs in some downward-sliding mournful language. It is not for her. There is a noticeboard on the far wall that is pinned with printed papers and notes which contain no threats. A central table is tumbled over with what look like boxes of games – you only need games if there are children. There is an ugly vase, too, that holds a thick, coloured shout of wild flowers, ungainly and extraordinarily moving.

Tang.

A muscular front door is propped open and gives sight of a sweeping …

Veranda, vestibule … The floor of an entrance of … Porch. Is the word porch?

There is a grey stone balustrade, bow-fronted steps like frozen stages in a liquid advance and then a sleeping garden, a broad approach of mossy gravel, gates. A bicycle dozes on its side beneath a tree. It does not indicate anything disturbing. And she should be checking for ways to leave here, routes between the shrubs, positions of fences and walls. *Does the bicycle work? Can it be made to?* Instead she passes by, locked in the track of sound from the piano, pressing deeper into the ground floor of the house, because too much sleep and cleanliness has ruined her good sense.

Tang.

The notes work in her chest like soft blows, something delivered by a child.

Tang.

And here a high, dark door lies open, the threshold framed in a dark wood, and she steps through.

The piano.

It really is.

Big room. Smells of oldness and summers and polish.

A piano.

The walls and ceiling are panelled in the same dully glowing timber. Close the door and you'd be shut up in a box.

It is too big to be a coffin and there's never the time for coffins and what use are they? The dead don't mind, it's the living who can't rest.

In one corner, a number of folded tables leans dimly. In another, she can see an accumulation of chairs, a scarf huddled on top of one stack, gentle and striped in colours and lost.

And the piano. Grand piano.

It's as black as death and night and boots, as the gleam of leather and the dark of eyes and mouths.

Its broad belly curves towards her, flawless.

Lyre … lyre post … top board, pedal, pedal, pedal … key bed … A piano still living.

There is thick silence now, perhaps her fault.

I have disturbed him.

A man who has lived to be old is sitting at the keys. Near his feet is a cloth roll that displays an ordered spread of clever instruments.

Tuning hammer, tuning fork, wedges, temperament strip.
Setting the bearings.

He has pushed his glasses up to rest over his forehead in exactly the way that living people do.

Sharp of pure, flat of pure …

He looks at her. He sees her.

Not for such a time …

Her face, she understands, is no longer within her control.

Setting the temperament, pure and wide of pure to make something perfect out of … strands of … spreads of …

She opens her mouth, reveals the dark of it, but says nothing. One of her hands makes a shape in the air.

And the man nods.

Her face, she is sure, is crawling and running with insects. A high breeze from somewhere is shaking her body and muffling her breath.

As if this is normal, he turns his head from her, gives her privacy, and sets his hands above the keys. She fights to stay still. She says one word in her mind, the one which has been the most useless.

Please.

But, as a reply to her, he plays.

Please.

He plays rivulets and ladders and wings in the air, sails over waters and breathing, living breath.

He plays the way it is to be alive.

He plays as if he owns the melody and has brought it with him because it could not be taken away. It has been possible for him to do that.

She has never heard it before and she maybe can't know melodies any more, but her body recognises the sense of it. And so she has to sit, has to sit on the bare boards like a child, child, girl child, sink down and be on the bare boards and feel the music rushing on them and touching her and soaking her and this is, this is, touching, this is the truth about knowing a hand for ever, this is a brush of fingers, this is remembering a face, this is the horror of remembering a face and this is holding and this is the hope and the desire and this is the need, this is loving a face, loving, this is loving, this is loving, this is the need, the touching, touching, palms, skin, lips, the wishing only to see a face again while the wood under your body howls and the air around your body howls and this is the truth about being still here.

The man knows and he has made her know. She is still alive.

It will be terrible, this surviving.

WE HAVE NOW

KAT DAY

I gaze at the jigsaw pieces scattered across the Formica tabletop. All the pieces are marked with shades of grey and black and white, but enough of the image is there that I'm able to recognise it. It's the birds across the top edge that give it away. Dad's done the outside first, of course. That's how you do jigsaws, isn't it? You find the corners, then you put the edges together, and then you build inwards.

Dad's head is bent over the table in concentration, sparse white hair forming a half-circle around his scalp. He doesn't speak. He doesn't often say much these days. But sometimes he comes back for a few moments, so I keep trying.

He's always liked M. C. Escher. It's a maths thing, I suppose. He used to tell me that there were Escher prints on the walls in his old school, and he would stand and stare at them for ages. Especially that one with the stairs that seem to be always going uphill. *You see, Annie*, he would say, *it's all about the way things repeat. The route might seem complicated, but eventually, we all end up back at the beginning.*

I watch him now. His fingers shiver and twitch, but they still have just enough precision to pick up the pieces. The room smells of warm air and overcooked food and disinfectant. I'm sitting on one of the chairs that match the table. They're old-fashioned, but not in a good way. Plastic, wipe-clean cushions and too-straight wood. I fidget, trying to get comfortable, and lean forward.

Dad slots another piece into place. It's part of the small cluster of houses nestled next to the river on the left-hand side of the picture. The same cluster is repeated on the right, but in darkness. That's the name of this print: *Day and Night*. At the top, the spaces in between the flock of black birds quietly morph into white birds, while the black birds fade into shadows.

A memory bubbles to the surface of my mind. 'Do you remember, Dad, when I moved out of Brailsford Road? Into that little flat?' He doesn't answer, but I didn't expect him to, really. 'There was no furniture in that flat,' I say. 'Not even a kettle. I had some things, but I'd left a lot behind at the house. You took one look around, put me in the van and drove me to that big furniture store. We came back with a bed and that chest of drawers – we've still got those, in the spare room – and a wardrobe. Loads of things. Then you stayed really late helping me put them all together.'

Dad frowns at the jigsaw. He's making good progress. The boats floating in a neat line on the daylight side of the river are all in place, and he's done a lot of the chequerboard field at the bottom. I pick up a piece with a windmill on it and slot it in. His head makes the smallest of movements. It might be a nod.

'Do you remember when you threw one of the Allen keys across the room?' I continue. '"I bloody hate this flat-pack crap!" you yelled. It bounced off a box and landed in my mug of tea. And we both stared at it, and then I said, "Bet you can't do that on purpose."'

He looks up at me then. There's a flicker of something in his eyes. A tiny flame trying to find enough oxygen to burn.

'And you said, "Tell you what: if I can, you have to pay me back for all this stuff," and I said, "I'm going to pay you back anyway, Dad," and you said, "Is it a deal?" And then you spent the next half-hour chucking Allen keys across the room. You missed every time. And my tea went cold.' I laugh.

Dad looks down again. He picks up a jigsaw piece that is mostly black and drops it into place. I reach out and touch his hand. The skin is loose and marked with age spots, but for a moment I feel like a little girl again, wriggling my fingers in Daddy's big, strong hand. He was my anchor, the thing that would always hold me safe.

He smiles. I'm not sure if it's anything to do with me.

I lapse into silence and for a while we both study the remaining pieces in their different greys, looking for their rightful places. We pick them up and put them down again. Recreating order from the jumble. Until, eventually, there it is. The last piece. It's mostly the wing of one of the white birds. It presses into place with a tiny *shhnick* sound.

Dad claps his hands together. 'Done it!' he says, and then he looks at me, and the spark in his eyes really *has* caught light, for a while. 'Oh, Annie, I didn't know you were here,' he says. 'Look, I've finished the jigsaw!'

'You have,' I agree, smiling.

He stares at the finished picture. It's glossy, and the reflection of the overhead lights make white spots on its surface. The pads of his fingers dance over it, like a blind man reading Braille.

He reaches the edge and I see him slide his hand under the fragile interlocking pieces. I reach out to stop him.

'No, Dad, don't break it.'

'I have to, Annie,' he says. His voice surprisingly firm. 'It won't fit back in the box like this.'

'I know,' I say, blinking. 'But we don't have to put it away yet. Let's look at it for a bit.'

My hand rests on his. Dad was wrong, I think. It's not about going back to the beginning. It's about appreciating the bit in the middle, when things are not quite one thing but they're not yet the other, either.

So we sit, and we watch the white birds turn back into the scenery around the black, and the black birds fade into the darkness around the white.

And we enjoy what we have now.

WE REHOUSE YOU

by Barney Farmer

A POEM FOR ALL THOSE WONDERING WHAT IT'S ALL ABOUT

MURRAY LACHLAN YOUNG

Please listen very carefully,
for taken hypothetically,
supported comprehensively,
basically, originally,
a single singularity
exploded quite impressively,
expanded exponentially,

creating stars and galaxies
with what must be quite logically
and coolly cosmologically
the building blocks of you and me
and continents and land and sea

A process evolutionary
through dinosaur hegemony
into our human ancestry
to cultural diversity

A growing global family
producing universities,
facilities, laboratories

Religion met the sciences
where people made discoveries
of fundamental articles
and elementary particles,
both magical and technical
and also mathematical

and random and symmetrical,
chemical and classical,
explained the metaphysical
that all things were divisible

But there must be a particle
much smaller than a neutron ball,
when answering the Hadron call
will finally inform us all
that we are one and we are all

That we are great and we are small
We are day and we are night
We are dark and we are light
I am he
As you are he
As you are me

As we are now and never

I am the mammoth
I am the dodo
I am the narwhal

Boo boo be doo!

SHIFA'

YASMINA FLOYER

When I saw you, you were unconscious by the side of the main road not far from my home. Traffic and people rushed past, but nobody noticed you. What was left of the snow from the week before had hardened into ice. It wasn't late but already dark, and people must have wanted to get back to the warm bodies waiting for them. I noticed the lump of your body interrupting the smooth line of pavement just beyond the light's reach, the neck of the street lamp craned over like a soldier standing guard. I couldn't tell from my window if anything about you was broken or not.

I don't like to go out. I told you that when I handled you carefully and took you back with me. I didn't think you could hear me, but they say that even when unconscious, words can pierce through the black. So I told you that this was the first time I had been out in four days. My words were not English, but I felt you knew my meaning.

The heating took a while to click on, so I placed you on the counter on top of a couple of sheets of kitchen towel next to the open oven door. I was saving the heating for Saturday, it was only Wednesday, but I knew that you needed it. Your eyes were neither shut nor open. I rubbed my numb hands together and crouched low to get a good look at you.

In the harsh light from above the counter I could just about make out the blue-green tint to your black feathers. They were dirty. I touched the point of your beak and you trembled. *It's OK*, I told you, *I am here.*

I had no way of telling if you were a boy or girl, but I named you Anas. It is a boy's name; it means 'affection'. I told you that I am Souzan. My name means 'burning flame'. I named you for the boy I once loved, before I came here. He was studying to be a doctor and I was to be a teacher. He was a couple of years older than me and we lived not far from one another. Our fathers were childhood friends, so we often spent evenings in one another's houses. His eyes were green like the colour that hides in your feathers. He wrote me letters and hid them in my books. Even now, when I see a book, I have to hold it by the back cover and shake the pages until I am certain that nothing will fall out. I even do it with newspapers sometimes. You must have thought me very silly when I told you this, but I wanted to believe that the books held a magic that would carry his words across the ocean to me. There had to be magic in this place. How else to explain the food that appears on the other side of my door?

I still think of him. Every day I imagine him in his house, sitting at the table with a small glass of freshly boiled coffee. His door, like the others in the village, is open to let in the morning sun. From where he is sitting, the sunlight picks up the red-brown in his black hair. He drops in a sugar cube and stirs. I watch him take a sip and wait for him to feel my eyes from the doorway. Finally, he looks up and smiles. I can see myself smiling back in the round glass of his spectacles. I try really hard to picture myself walking across the room to him, but each time I try, my mind gets stuck.

Other times I envisage him here, in this place. I pretend it is bigger. The counter that you slept on that first night becomes a kitchen in a room of its own. The mattress on the floor against the far wall is our bedroom. The bathroom in the hall is not shared by anyone but the two of us. That is how I picture it. I look at the front door whenever I hear others coming into the building. The heavy slam of the main door and light footsteps running up to the first floor where I sit listening become his steps. I hear keys and can see him in my thoughts from the other side of the door. He is holding a fresh loaf of flat bread and a yellow hibiscus that he will tuck behind my ear as soon as he comes in. But then I am back on this side of the door, and the footsteps are gone and I can't make myself see him any more.

There have been knocks. They start out as light taps then become so hard that the door shakes. I ignore them because I know it is not him. I have to think of him like this, in his kitchen, or coming up these stairs. It stops me from thinking about what I left behind.

That day the air in the village cracked louder than thunder and the sky was darkened with solid black clouds that rose from the ground. I didn't look back to see what had become of his street. I didn't look up to see what was falling from the sky. With so many dead, we stopped belonging to separate families and became bound to one another, moving with a single purpose. I added my voice to the bassline of grief that followed us as we left the village. I did not look back once.

So when I brought you home, you became my Anas, my little love. That first night, I didn't know what to give you, so I tore up a slice of bread and dipped it in milk, leaving the soggy pieces by your beak, watching as it soaked into the kitchen paper. You closed your eyes.

I wondered what you were thinking of. Were you dreaming of home? Yes, I think you must have been. That is what we all think of when we are in pain, isn't it, Anas? Home. I like to think that your home is not far from where I grew up. I remember as a little girl watching a clear sky filled with so many of you moving as a single quivering cloud; pulling one way then shifting inwards like a sand dune. You must miss them. Your kind is not made to be alone.

I didn't sleep that first night. I sat with you and prayed. I wanted to stroke you and give you a small kiss, but I was worried I would hurt you. When the sun rose and your eyes were still shut, I believed you had gone. But then your eyes opened. The bread remained untouched. Small flies circled a brown banana not far from you. I sat very still with my palms cupped above the oversweet smell. I waited until they sat, five in my right hand, fingers closing slowly until I had them all. I left them by your head and when I came back from washing my hands they were gone.

You looked too big to be a fledging, but you were still small. I decided you were a teenager, so not much younger than me. You drank water from the lid of a plastic bottle. It was bright orange like the sunset. I wanted something near you to remind you of the sky. I only look at the sky through the thin glass of my window. Sometimes when it looks empty outside, I will lean my head out into the cool breeze and breathe in deeply.

A few weeks ago I rode the night bus back from the office that I clean. The evening still held some of the day's heat, so I got off a few stops early, wanting to feel the last of the dry leaves under my feet. I didn't notice them at first. There were two of them. They were laughing and calling out, but I didn't think they were speaking to me. Then I felt a tug at the back of my head. One of them had my scarf in his hand and I could feel it slipping, my black hair coming loose. I turned on them, said, 'Please.' They laughed some more, calling out, 'Please, please.'

They were shouting at me to go home. I wanted nothing more than to do that. The one who had hold of my scarf then had hold of my hair, gripping it in his fist.

Some of it lifted away in his fingers and I could feel cool blood seeping across my scalp. The other man kicked my legs. I was on the floor and they kicked and kicked until they grew bored and then left me there.

You see my mouth, Anas? Look, I will show you. This is where my tooth hung on by a thread of gum before I pulled it out. I used to have a beautiful smile. I can say that now without sounding immodest, because it is not something I will ever get back. It is good that he can't see me now. You don't mind though, do you? I can't help smiling around you.

It wasn't long until you began to eat the bread, maybe only a couple of days. I shook the can of coins that used to hold red beans, then counted out what was left. Then there was a knock at the door. I waited more than ten minutes until I was sure we were alone. When I opened it, there was some milk and bread in a bag, just like there had been a few days before that. I looked down the hall and towards the stairwell, and couldn't see anybody. I came back to you, opened the packet and counted out slices of bread instead.

You have been with me for ten days. Your wings are strong. I know that you love me but love your family more. I sit with my hands cupped, palms up, until, finally, you land on them, your restless feet scratching my skin like needles. I close my hands and tuck you into my shawl. We go outside, past the bicycles in the hall and the strollers under the stairwell. The main door is heavier than I remember. We make our way out and across the small patch of green and then cross the big road.

This is where I found you. The ice is gone. I thought that perhaps you would be still and look at me, that I would need to throw you back into the sky, but when I open my shawl you are gone. Goodbye, my Anas, be happy.

I walk back knowing I won't hear the sound of your chatter bounce off my walls when I get in. When I arrive at my door, there is a woman, knocking gently. I watch her knock harder, and then stop. She places a plastic bag down then turns.

'Oh, it's you. Hello. I'm from upstairs. I hope you don't mind me …' she says, pointing to the bag of milk and bread, '… only I saw you come in a few weeks ago from my window. You didn't seem in a good way.'

I don't catch all her words, but her meaning makes its way to me. 'I'm Helen.'

She holds out her hand. Her face is soft and lined. Her smile reaches the corners of her eyes. She says nothing more, simply waits and smiles, hand outstretched. I see a thin gold band hugged by the doughy flesh of her fingers.

When I take her hand in mine, she doesn't let go. I take a step towards her, spreading my other hand over my chest, and pat gently.

'Souzan.'

PEACE

DAISY BUCHANAN

'I have a surprise for you!' Mum announced as I walked into the kitchen.

I've heard these words enough over my lifetime to feel apprehension bordering on dread whenever she utters them. The summer I turned eighteen, the 'surprise' was that she had arranged a six-week walking pilgrimage to Walsingham for me, and she'd already told my friends that they would have to find someone else to take my place on the Thomas Cook flight to Kavos. Just before I got married, her great news was that our old parish priest, then ninety-three, had agreed to conduct the ceremony as a favour, even though my husband and I are filthy heathens, and that we could go ahead and cancel the register office. (She'd tried to ring up and do it herself, but the man on the phone wouldn't let her talk on our behalf. Thank goodness for bureaucracy.) But the first, and worst, Catholic surprise that I remember happened shortly after my thirteenth birthday.

It was the third day of the Easter holidays. I'd been sleeping over at my unsuitable friend Faye's. Faye terrified me slightly, but I revelled in our friendship because she was an only child, her mum was never overly concerned about her whereabouts and she knew how to grill her own fish fingers. Faye rarely saw her dad, and didn't seem to mind much, and I was vaguely envious that there wasn't anyone in her life to tell her off for not practising her clarinet or stacking the dishwasher properly.

Faye's mum was out for the evening, and she'd left us some cash to order a takeaway pizza. I studied the menu with intense, attempted sophistication. 'Gosh, *pineapple?* Maybe we should have that. And *an-anchovy.*' Bizarrely, I pronounced the unfamiliar word '*un-huffy*' thinking anything exotic and unfamiliar should have a vaguely Latinate ring. A juan-chovy.

Faye looked profoundly bored. 'Whatever. I don't care. Hey, you know what we *should* do? I just saw this on TV!' Her eyes gleamed, and she produced a bottle of Quink ink and a compass. I stared at her. Faye had never knowingly cared about stationery. I'd seen her throw a protractor in the wastepaper bin, eyeing it with disdain. 'What the fuck will I ever need this bendy ruler for?' Did Faye want to get a head start on our holiday homework? This seemed unlikely.

'You can do tattoos at home! You just need ink and a needle. It's what they did for sailors in the olden days!' she said proudly.

Lamely, I could only think of one objection. 'But you've got blue ink! Aren't most tattoos supposed to be black?'

She shrugged. 'Navy blue looks black, basically. I'll just have to use loads of ink. Where do you want it?'

Ideally, on someone else's body was where I wanted it. But arguing with Faye was just like arguing with my parents, albeit with a very different result. They said what they wanted, you expressed your opposing views, and they did it their way anyway.

I thought about my bum. No one would ever, ever see my bum, and I'd already decided that in the unlikely event that a boy ever wanted to have sex with me, I'd do lots of strategic walking backwards and somehow erotically conceal myself with a large bath sheet. But there was no way I'd get my bum out for Faye. I didn't trust her not to take a picture and circulate it around the school.

'What about your arm?' she said, hopefully. 'There's lots of space on the top.'

In my head, I travelled in time to summer and sadly imagined my inking sticking out of my T-shirt sleeve. Then I had a brainwave. 'What about on my foot?' I suggested. 'Nice flat surface, lots of space, and I can just stop wearing sandals!'

Faye looked slightly hurt by the idea that I'd want to hide her artwork from the world, but she got over it. 'What do you want me to do? I know! A dolphin!'

I'd seen a girl in the sixth form with a dolphin tattoo on her shoulder, and it seemed fairly conventional and respectable. So I made Faye practise dolphins on a bit of A4 printer paper, until we both decided to give it up as a bad job. Faye could not get the tail right.

'We need something simple but classic. Something easy. A logo.' Her eyes travelled to my black leather school bag, which she had graffitied with Tippex peace signs. 'Yes! Why didn't I think of that before! And with the compass we can draw a circle, and I'll just fill it in!'

Faye buried the needle of the compass in my foot, and I yelped in pain, so she ran to the fridge for a wine bottle and drew around it. Then she forgot exactly how they did home-made tattoos on TV. She dipped the compass in ink, and then punctured my skin. It hurt horribly and drew a little blood but made no permanent dark mark. So she tipped some ink over my foot and stabbed rapidly and repeatedly, hoping the scab would turn into a tattoo. This was when I started crying silently, and she told me that I was making my foot wobble and suggested that I anaethetise myself by downing the contents of the wine bottle. At some point, she found the blade of an old-fashioned letter opener. At some point I passed out. I think Faye continued working.

When I woke up, it was morning. My foot appeared to have recently stopped bleeding. Faye was awake, and proud. 'I put some Savlon on it, so it should be healed up now. What do you think?'

The design on my foot was unmistakably a peace sign. It was bright blue in places, grey in others, and quite scabby, but no one could dispute the fact that Faye had done what she had set out to do. My foot looked slightly swollen and felt very painful.

'Yeah, they said it would hurt on the programme,' Faye claimed, breezily. 'It should be all right in a week. Oooh, we didn't order pizza!'

She pocketed the twenty quid, and I felt aggrieved.

Faye's mum appeared to have left for work – if she came home at all – so we walked to the park to throw the wine bottle in a public bin, Faye deflecting saucy suggestions from boys with cigarettes as I limped behind her. My mum picked me up after lunch and announced her surprise. I was still young and hopeful enough to believe it might be McDonald's for tea, or even that she'd given it some thought and decided that we could have Sky telly and it wouldn't necessarily make us fail our exams.

'Father Larry was looking for volunteers for the Maundy Thursday foot washing, so I've put you forward! He's delighted – they don't usually get the younger folk. You'll have to go early this evening, and sit at the front so you can get to the altar. That's exciting, isn't it?!'

I opened my mouth and took a shallow, rapid intake of breath. 'But I was going to … do … some homework! What about little Roisin! She'd be adorable!'

Mum shook her head. 'They're not having kiddies after they tried it a few years ago with the Sunday School and wrecked Sister Victoire's crepe-paper triptych. Apparently Barbara Sullivan's little boy technically had trench foot. It's an honour! You should be pleased!'

We arrived at home and I got out of the Corsa, smiling and wincing as I wrenched my tender foot out of the vehicle. I landed on it and made an odd noise. 'Woooaaaaarghhhh-OH!'

Mum frowned. 'Did you do something to your leg?'

'Ah, hahahaha, um, no. I was just laughing! Thinking about the triptych.'

Mum looked cross. 'People worked *very* hard on that triptych.'

I *had* to find my little sister Catherine, and I had to make her forget that, shortly before I'd left for Faye's, I'd called her 'a sad stinky virgin with a smelly front bum'. I had very little to bribe her with – my piggy bank contained £24.78. I'd start at a tenner and my two newest bottles of nail polish, and maybe throw in a read of my diary. I found her, biro-ing a moustache on one of Roisin's Barbies.

'Catherine, Mum is making me have my feet washed at Mass, and I really don't want to. Swap with me. I'll pay you?'

Catherine did not look up. 'No.'

'*Please!*'

She raised her head just enough to get a good look at my right sock, which was beginning to bear a faint, bloody peace sign. 'What in the name of actual Christ have you done?' She swiped at the sock. I tried to move out of the way, but she was too quick for me. I blinked tears away. You did not show weakness in front of Catherine.

'Please don't tell Mum,' I begged.

Catherine smirked. 'No need. It's going to be much more

fun to watch her reaction tonight – and watch you squirm in the meantime.'

The full significance of her words hit me a full four hours later, when, sitting in front of a bowl full of water, in full view of the congregation, I peeled off my right sock.

There was an audible gasp. I looked down and saw my peace sign as if for the first time. It had started bleeding again. My mother stood up, and I felt overwhelmed by a rush of nausea.

'Margaret Maria Frances, WHAT HAVE YOU DONE TO YOURSELF?'

A full five seconds passed. Mum apologised, and we carried on. Father Larry murmured something, and plunged my foot into the bowl of lukewarm water, an action that was immensely soothing. I decided to enjoy the relative peace of the Mass, knowing that the journey home, and the rest of my life, would be full of recriminations and accusations.

'The Mass is ended! Go in peace to love and serve the Lord,' said Father Larry.

As I'd predicted, there was nothing peaceful about it. From the passenger seat of the Corsa, Mum muttered, 'Never been so ashamed!' and, 'Mortified, in front of the parish!' and, 'I never believed my own daughter could … could … WHERE WAS THAT CHILD'S MOTHER, ANYWAY?' and, 'You're not to see Faye again.'

'Good!' I hissed, too afraid to say out loud, 'Faye is a bitch and I hate her.' I did want to see her again. I wanted her to take full responsibility for her crimes. Her mum never shouted at her. I was never, ever as naughty as she was – and all my mum did was shout at me.

By Sunday, Mum was still angry. 'You don't deserve this!' she said at breakfast, aggressively plonking a box in front of me, which contained a Thornton's Easter egg, on which a shop assistant had iced my name, Maggie, inside a heart. At lunch, I was allowed a small glass of wine, and the rest of the family were allowed to talk to me.

'You have to admit, it was hilarious when Mum stood up,' said Catherine.

Roisin added, 'Actually, Mummy, none of us will have tattoos now, because Maggie has put us off! So this is a good thing!'

I kicked her under the table, and my scab twinged.

Before the end of the holidays, Mum took me to see Doctor Goyal, who told us that Faye's work was permanent, but it would heal, and I wasn't going to die prematurely or need to have my foot amputated as a result. I spent less time with Faye, who eventually left school and went off to college. I became very fond of my slightly scabby peace sign, and told its origin story to the various men in my life, most of whom I managed to have satisfactory congress with, which didn't require any complicated tricks with towels. I even thought about having the work professionally inked over on my thirtieth birthday.

Mum announced her latest surprise shortly after she turned sixty. I wasn't expecting it to be life-altering – after all, she'd finally agreed to getting Sky TV when I left to go to university. I assumed she was dragging Dad to Lourdes, or that the Catholic Women's League were finally getting their own building after being forced to hold their meetings in the church hall annexe.

'Look!' she announced, gamely kicking her right leg in the air.

I looked. She didn't usually paint her toenails. I didn't recognise that tan leather sandal. But these didn't seem like surprises worthy of announcement, and they weren't.

'No, look again!' she said, with another kick.

Then I saw it. Just above her three middle toes, there was a small, neat black circle bisected by a bold line, with two smaller, diagonal lines intersecting it.

'Mum! You didn't!'

She looked pleased, and slightly sheepish. 'Some of the Catholic Women were talking about doing it for their birthdays – it started as a joke, and then ...' She hugged me, and we both started crying. 'I was so mean to you! You were just a child! You didn't know what you were doing! And who cares what your feet look like anyway!' She started giggling. 'This will make you laugh. The man who did it told me that to keep it moisturised, I have to put your dad's Preparation H on it!'

That night, I managed to find Faye on Facebook. She appeared to be studying for a biology Ph.D. at Birmingham university, and she had a son. I sent her a message about Mum, telling her how funny I found it, how happy it made me, and how much I missed her. Being loved simply isn't the same as being understood, and I felt as though Mum had loved me for my whole life, but she'd just started to understand me. I wondered whether Faye's mum made her feel enough of either when she was growing up, and I wished I'd made a greater effort to do the same for her. But, as I signed off with three kisses, I thought, *It's never too late*.

CELIA CITIZEN

L. A. CRAIG

Celia Butler – senior citizen. A former Miss Scarborough, widow to a lighthouse keeper, and now – for my sins – chief honcho of Neighbourhood Watch on the Shaftoe Estate.

Like I've nothing better to be doing (folk think we retired types spend all day on our backsides, dunking Hobnobs and spouting crown green bowls). But – I won't have anyone say I don't do my bit.

Our Nigel, who can't find a 'window' for his own mother any other time, insists on dropping me off at the monthly conflab. Strides into the community centre, shaking hands like a native when, truth is, he thought he was too good for the place the minute he'd grown out of Lego. No, his preferred abode is a converted shoe factory with a view of some old gasworks. Calls it *loft living*. I ask you … On the rare occasion a suit from the council shows their face, Nigel's in his element.

'Celia's son. Pleasure to meet you.'

Obviously thinks my status will get him somewhere.

Kids these days don't need to brown-nose. They can start a business from their pushchair with this interweb and Twitterfy. What's the word? Dynamic. Multibillionaires by the time they're twenty-seven. And good luck to them, I say. Personally, I've a lot in common with the youngsters. Love their fashionable clobber too – you know, leggings and a smocky top that covers my thighs. Skims the unmentionables but enhances what I've still got left.

Decent pins, as my late husband use to say. And Ugg boots. So comfy. You can keep your Clarks' wide-fit.

Six times a week (too busy to commit any more), I do a walkabout of the whole estate, and if that's not good enough, I'm perfectly happy to abdicate.

The silver-haired queue waits for nine-thirty. Bus-pass kick-off.

'Morning, Audrey. Stan. You've got the weather for it.'

For what, I've no idea, but they seem pleased I've noticed. 'Couldn't ask for better,' Stan pipes back.

'Enjoy it while it lasts.'

Empty talk. But when you're head of Neighbourhood Watch people expect an acknowledgement, so then it's called *community spirit*.

When we first moved here, there was a fishmonger, newsagent, butcher, and a mini Spar. Now the Spar's knocked through to the newsagent's. The fishmonger's is a hairdresser's and the butcher's – a tattoo shop called Tat Cat. A solid bald man stands outside, the leg of his sweatpants rolled up to his groin, smoking.

'Mind if I look at your … artwork?'

'Go for it,' he says. Thrusts a hefty thigh closer to my glasses. A strip of his leg is shaved, the skin baby pink where the needle's stabbed a hundred times, and a paper towel tucked into his trouser leg flaps in the breeze.

'It's an all-seeing eye,' he explains.

'Very useful.'

'Stings like fuck.' He sucks his ciggie, blows the smoke behind.

Sometimes you have to ignore the language.

'Been pondering over one myself,' I say. It's more of a daydream, but it gives me something to talk about. 'A butterfly, on my ankle.'

'Nice one, grandma.'

'But, you know – what with the expense … A pension doesn't stretch far these days. Maybe I'll persuade my son to treat me for Christmas.'

'Sick.'

'My sentiments exactly.'

He flicks his cigarette to the pavement. 'Time for round two.'

'Yes, must crack on myself. Good luck with … the pain and everything.'

Once he's back inside, I deposit his cigarette butt in the bin located less than a sneeze away. Usually I would ask if a person's mother taught them to drop litter, but in this job, it's wise to let the odd thing go for the sake of good relations.

Past the shops, houses that used to be council, but now they're all glass porches, extensions, front gardens paved over to drives. At the one with silver-tipped railings, loading bikes onto a roof rack: three gents in skimpy Lycra. People say men their age should know better. Tommyrot. In my opinion, a snug silhouette held in place where gravity would normally fail it, is a rather handsome sight.

'Lovely morning for a ride.'

'Room for a little one,' says the tallest.

'If it wasn't for my dicky knee, I'd be in there like a shot.'

'Phil!' he shouts to the one wheeling his bike down the path. 'Got a lassie here needs your magic hands.'

The one called Phil stops. Leans his bike against the wall, blows into his palms and rubs them together. Wiggles his fingers.

'You just keep your hands on the handlebars.'

'Where's the fun in that?'

We giggle.

'Sure you won't join us?' asks his friend.

'Maybe next time,' I say. 'My Lycra's in the wash.'

A bit of banter cheers you up, doesn't it? A slice of silly for the soul. Like me last night – cha-cha-ing to 'Cherry Pink and Apple Blossom White' in the bathroom mirror. Starkers, apart from my face pack.

The kids at the skate park are in show-off mode, pulling tricks in Day-Glo laces and baggy tops. The spangled-up brigade pose round the edges, as if on their marks for a party. Huddles and cliques. Who fancies who?

A concrete bunker churning with adolescence. It brings back memories of seaside larks, intense crushes – first kisses. Teenagers drunk with the freedom of school holidays. Little do they know it's a feeling they'll chase for the rest of their lives.

I could watch all day. But – duty calls.

It's not often I use my notepad (flowery, and full of forgetful-old-lady notes – wink wink), but this van here looks a tad shifty.

White with rusted trim. Back doors splayed wide.

And inside: a bed. An open box of cornflakes. Three screwdrivers. A crowbar.

Hardly enough equipment for a self-employed Avon lady, never mind a tradesperson. Writing on the side of the van has been scrubbed out. Strange. Any *legit* business would surely advertise their services.

Unless they have a *reason* to be incognito.

I'm not happy about this. At all.

As I scribble down the number plate with my engraved

Paper Mate (*I ♥ Neighbourhood Watch*) – another 'thoughtful' Christmas gift from our Nigel – this young chap comes up. All butter-wouldn't-melt-a-choirboy face.

I'm about to ask if he knows the owner's whereabouts, when he sidles right up to my shoulder. And with all the vile menace of Beelzebub, spits, 'Had a good look, missus?'

It takes a few seconds to compose myself; his angelic face and filthy attitude are such a confusing mismatch.

'Don't know what you mean,' I say, determined not to wobble. 'I only stopped to check my shopping list.'

'And I reckon you've got your nose *right* in my business.'

'Well, you're entitled to your opinion, but I assure you—'

He slams the left door, the right. Jabs his finger a whisper away from the tip of my nose. 'People like you wanna get a life.'

But before I get the chance to compare my experiences in life to his lack of hot dinners, the impudent wee beggar jumps behind the wheel.

Zooms off.

Three doors down, Biddy McCarthy clashes two empty wine bottles in her recycling. The deep V-neck of her dressing gown clamped shut with a clothes peg to cover her bony chest. 'Did you hear that cheek?' I say, desperate to vent to someone.

'Sorry, Celia.' She half waves, half ignores me. 'Need to rescue my bath.'

'Practically accused me of …'

But Biddy's front door is shut.

It's always the same.

When it comes to confrontation, no one wants to know.

Get a life.

It's the 'go-to' phrase, isn't it? Don't bother to actually enquire about a person's life instead of insulting them all over the place. You do your best to keep the estate pleasant, give up your valuable time … Rotten apples always leave a sour taste.

Any other day, I scoot past the fence to the allotments, don't bother going inside. Cabbages, rhubarb, makeshift scarecrows. Hardly a den of iniquity. Mind you, if they *were* growing any of that weedyamacallit, I'd sniff it out in a shot. Today, the gentle cluck-clucking lures me.

Hen Hut was dreamed up by the Residents' Association. To help older folk without families. Give them something to care for, a reason to get up every day. Meet others in the same boat, have a chinwag, that sort of thing.

I'll just show my face.

The crazy-paved path winds down past rows of shabby and showroom veg to a square of perfectly mown lawn, honey-coloured wicker chairs, a summerhouse with pastel bunting, wafting coffee. An oasis of chatter and hen warble.

Mr Banerjee is painting a hutch sky blue.

'Well, good morning, Celia,' he says. 'You here on official business, or is this a social call?'

'Bit of both,' I say. 'Thought I'd come for a gander, see what you've done with the place.'

He swoops out his arm, as if inviting me into a stately home. 'Fancy a cuppa?'

'Go on, then, just a quick one before I press on.'

'No resting for the wicked, eh?'

A huge ginger bird scuffs around our feet. He scoops it up. 'This one's Joy. Stroke her if you like.'

'She won't peck?'

'Are you kidding? She'll probably fall asleep.'

He takes my hand. 'Here, like this.' Smoothes it gently down the warm feathers of Joy's breast. Scattering all thoughts of rotten apples.

Half-a-dozen other hens pick at the grass, snooze in the laps of grateful seniors. 'Do they all have names?'

'Absolutely. We've got Mabel, Geraldine, Esther, Aretha. And the one over there' – he points to a speckled specimen – 'is Dumbledore.' He shakes his head. 'Don't ask. Wilton Road Primary School named it.'

When he laughs, I notice his teeth. Still his own. I admire a man with standards in oral hygiene. He carefully places Joy back on the grass.

'Most people only see a silly bird,' he says, eyes all wistful. 'But you become close – like friends.' And then he beams that sparkly smile again. 'Need all the friends we can get at our time of life, eh?'

'Well, personally mine's chock full …'

'Samir.'

'Samir,' I repeat to brown eyes focused on mine. They remind me of a certain lighthouse keeper.

'Of course' – he puts a hand on my arm for a brief second – 'they're no substitute for the real thing.'

'Of course.'

I'd almost forgotten how it feels to blush. 'You've got it nice here,' I say.

'All mod cons: microwave, fridge, CD player. And on summer nights, Josie brings her karaoke machine for a sing-song. Fairy lights twinkling, glass of Baileys or three,' he chuckles. 'It's like a Hawaiian beach bar.'

'Sounds perfect.'

An absolute riot compared to being slumped in front of *EastEnders* in a Marks & Spencer onesie. Tucked up with Maeve Binchy by nine-thirty.

'Sit.' He pulls over a comfy chair. 'Relax a while.'

As I take the weight off, something about his kindness

makes neighbourhood obligations seem unimportant.

'Do you take sugar?'

And for the first time in a long while, engrossed in genuine, heartfelt conversation, a whole afternoon simply fritters away.

THE GOOD SANDYMAN

MIKE GAYLE

Tyson was conflicted.

The meal his mum had just presented him with – fried egg and big fat oven chips slathered in tomato ketchup – was his most favourite in the entire world. It was the meal he asked for if he'd been ill for a few days and his mum offered to make something special to cheer him up. It was the meal he chose if he'd got a good school report and his mum asked him what he wanted for a treat. It was the meal he'd already made up his mind he would eat twice a week when he was a grown-up (more than that and it wouldn't feel like a treat any more) and lived on his own. And when Ajay told him that his dad said that in America if you kill someone and get caught, you get to eat one last meal before they kill you back, Tyson didn't doubt for a moment that fried egg and big fat oven chips slathered in tomato ketchup would be his.

And yet as much as he loved it, he loved being out on his bike just that little bit more, which could mean only one thing: the meal he normally savoured every mouthful of would have to be bolted down like it was plain old beans on toast. He couldn't risk wasting a single second. Ajay's mum had said that Ajay could only come out on his new bike for an hour after tea. An hour wasn't very long, especially when Tyson had to ride over to Ajay's first. An hour was nothing when there were new tricks to learn, games of tag-on-bike to play and jumps off the kerb to perfect. An hour wasn't any time at all. Tyson glanced at the chunky camouflage-pattern digital army watch he'd had for his last birthday and, with much sadness in his heart, wolfed down – in precisely one minute and fifty-nine point nine seconds – the meal his mum had lovingly prepared.

Tyson felt like his tummy might pop as he frantically pedalled away from the estate. On a good day it took about ten minutes to get to Ajay's house, but Tyson was convinced he could do it in eight if he tried hard enough. Zipping along the pavement in the last few hours of the summer sunshine, he dodged in and out of oncoming dog walkers, skilfully avoided glistening patches of broken glass and swerved around an upturned wheelie bin all with the dexterity of the expert rider he was. One day he would do this for a living, he told himself as he left the traffic-laden main road and turned off towards the much quieter Heeley Avenue. One day he would get paid money for being this good at riding his bike. He might even get his own YouTube channel teaching people how to be as good as he was at riding his bike.

In the middle of trying to decide whether Tysononbikes or Tysonbikes would be the best name for his YouTube show, Tyson felt a sharp pain in his side, as if he had just been hit by a laser beam. It hurt so much it brought tears to his eyes and he quickly came to a halt. He knew what the pain was: a stitch. The pain you get when you do too much exercise too soon after eating. Tyson's mum was always telling him to slow down and sit still after meals and he'd wait until she wasn't looking and roll his eyes. His mum worried too much. People who were really good on their bikes like he was didn't get a stitch.

Abandoning his bike on the pavement, Tyson stood contorting himself, trying to get into a position where the pain hurt the least. It took several poses, but eventually he discovered that putting his head between his legs while squeezing his eyes shut and breathing through his nose worked best. He tried hard not to cry while he did this, but then, in the middle of a particularly sharp jab of pain, something distracted him. It was a noise. Almost – what was the word? – a groan … a groan like when his sister Kaya caught a vomiting bug last winter and kept spewing everywhere. Afterwards she would groan just like that. Opening his eyes, Tyson stood up straight and turned in the direction of the noise. In front of him was a house that Tyson guesstimated to be a million times larger than the maisonette he lived in. The house had two large bay windows, a double garage with a white door, a yellow front door and in front of it all, a neatly kept lawn. In the middle of the lawn, wearing brown trousers and a checked shirt and lying in a funny position, was a white-haired old man.

Even though he was pretty sure it was the old man who was groaning, Tyson wondered if he was dead. Did dead people groan? He didn't think so.

Tyson looked around to see if there was a grown-up around who he could talk to about the old man, but there wasn't anyone. The street was deserted.

There were no cars or people in sight, just Tyson and a groaning old man.

Tyson wondered if it was some kind of trap. His mum was always telling him not to talk to strangers. Maybe this stranger had come up with a new way to talk to children. Maybe if he went to talk to him, the man would get up suddenly and grab him and then Tyson would be kidnapped, and he'd never get to see his mum or dad or sister again.

Tyson decided to test out his theory and called out to the old man, 'Are you trying to kidnap me?'

The old man didn't reply.

'Because if you are, I know kung fu, so I will be able to fight you off and when my dad finds out what you've done, he'll batter you.'

The old man still didn't respond.

Tyson didn't think the old man was a kidnapper. He thought that the old man was probably in trouble and needed help. A memory popped into Tyson's head: an assembly that Mr Manion, his school's deputy headmaster, gave last term. He couldn't remember much about it. A man got robbed. Different people passed by him and only one stopped to help and he was called the Good Sandyman.

It might have been the name, or the fact that he was helping people, but there was something about the Good Sandyman that made Tyson imagine him as a superhero like one of the characters in his dad's favourite comic books, with a cool costume and a special superpower. When he told this to Ajay, his friend laughed and told him that he was wrong. The Good Sandyman was just an ordinary man in a dressing gown and sandals like they used to wear in olden times and he didn't have any superpowers: he just went around doing nice things, a bit like Jesus.

After that Tyson forgot all about the Good Sandyman until this moment and now he could think of nothing else. Mr Manion had said everyone should be a Good Sandyman if they got the chance and Tyson thought that maybe this was his.

Still unsure whether or not he was about to be kidnapped, Tyson edged himself across the gravel drive – one scrunch at a time – ready to sprint away should the need arise. But the old man lay still and so he crept all the way over to the centre of the lawn until he was standing right over him.

'Are you dead?'

The old man's eyes flicked open and Tyson leapt back in surprise.

'Don't even think about trying to steal my wallet, you little oik,' said the old man. 'The police are on their way and I'll make sure they lock you up.'

Tyson didn't move. 'I don't want your smelly old wallet. I thought you were in trouble.'

'Well, I'm not,' said the old man. 'So just leave me alone and get off my property.'

Tyson wished he'd paid more attention to the story Mr Manion told about the Good Sandyman because he couldn't remember the part where the man who needed help told the only person who helped him to go away.

'Don't you need help?' asked Tyson.

'Not from you I don't,' said the old man. 'You're one of those kids from the estate, aren't you? I see your lot all the time. Coming round here causing trouble. One of you even tried to burgle my house! I'm not having it, I tell you, so clear off!'

Tyson took half a step back almost as if he expected the old man to lunge in his direction. But aside from producing a long thread of spit that dangled from his mouth to just above the ground, the old man didn't move a muscle.

'Are you sure you want me to go?' asked Tyson.

'That's what I said, didn't I?' snapped the old man.

'But there's no one else around to help you,' said Tyson.

'The day I need help from people like you,' said the old man, 'is the day they can drop me off at the knacker's yard.'

Tyson didn't know what a knacker's yard was, but he didn't imagine it was pleasant. 'Do you know what, old man?' said

Tyson, feeling a little bit like he might cry. 'You are not a very nice person at all. I was on my way to Ajay's because he's got a new bike and he's only got an hour to play out and I could be there right now instead of trying to help you.'

As Tyson stomped back to his bike he was pretty sure he heard the old man mutter something under his breath that wasn't very nice. He checked his watch and discovered that he'd wasted nearly five minutes of his Ajay time trying to help someone who didn't want to be helped. Tomorrow, Tyson decided, he was going to find Mr Manion and tell him that his stupid Sandyman story didn't work in real life because in real life old men were too mean to accept help from people who were only being nice. Tyson imagined that Mr Manion would be so impressed that he had tried to be like the Sandyman that he might even move him up the zone board. Currently Tyson was in red for talking when he should have been listening to what his teacher Miss Nightingale was telling the class about what life was like in Tudor times. Tyson tried to explain to Miss Nightingale that he was only telling Ajay how they used to throw buckets of poo and wee out of the window because they didn't have a sewer system in those days, but she wouldn't let him finish.

As Tyson cycled away from the old man, he felt like a huge weight had been lifted from his shoulders. The pain in his stomach was gone, his once-leaden legs felt lighter than air, and he had even convinced himself that if Ajay really begged and pleaded and promised to do some extra jobs for her, then his mum might let him stay out a little bit longer. All was not lost; they could still do everything they'd planned to do. That silly old man hadn't completely spoiled their evening.

Ajay's house was just a left at the end of the road onto Old Brook Avenue, then right all the way down Market Road, then left at Turnham Close and up the hill. If he rode as hard as he had been riding before he saw the old man he'd be there in under six minutes (maybe even five if he didn't get a stitch again). But at the end of the road Tyson did something he hadn't been expecting: he came to an abrupt stop and thought about the old man.

Tyson imagined the old man still lying where he'd found him. He imagined he probably wasn't very comfortable on the hard ground. He imagined that the old man might even need the loo, which would make him feel even more uncomfortable than he already was. Then he imagined that the old man was his great-granddad and the thought alone was enough to bring big, fat, hot, salty tears to his eyes. Tyson's great granddad was very old and lived in a home for old people, but he was one of the best people Tyson knew and he loved him very much. He did a really funny thing with his false teeth that made Tyson cry with laughter. Tyson didn't like the thought of his great-granddad lying on a hard lawn and maybe needing the toilet and not being able to go.

Tyson picked up his bike, turned it around on the spot and cycled back to the old man as fast as his legs would take him. When he reached the old man's house he put on his back brake so sharply that he skidded in a wide arc that was so cool he wished someone had recorded it on their phone for him. Leaping off his bike, Tyson ran to the old man, who was still lying in exactly the same spot.

'I've come back,' said Tyson.

'I told you to leave me alone,' said the old man in a different voice from the one he'd used before. This one was weaker, as if his batteries were beginning to run out.

'I know you did,' said Tyson. 'But I'm not going to listen to you. You need help.'

'I don't want your help,' said the old man in that same voice.

'And I don't really want to help you because you're not a very nice person,' said Tyson. 'But I'm going to anyway.'

'I said go away,' said the old man feebly, and then he did something that Tyson didn't expect: he started to cry. Not big tears like a baby. But small, quiet ones as if he was just really sad.

'It's not fair,' said the old man as Tyson watched tear after tear roll from his eyes on to the grass.

'What's not fair?' asked Tyson.

The old man blinked at Tyson and Tyson blinked right back. 'Getting old,' said the old man.

'There are lots of good things about being old,' said Tyson, sitting down on the ground next to the old man. 'Like, you don't have to go to work, and you get to know lots of stuff because you've been around so long … and … oh, yeah … no one cares if you fart really loudly – my great-granddad farts all the time and no one says anything, but when I do it my mum goes mental.'

The old man made a short wheezing rasp that Tyson concluded was either his last dying breath or an attempt at a laugh. The old man's face softened, granite turning into flesh and he lifted one of his huge, hairy hands shakily in the air.

'You want me to help you up?' asked Tyson.

The man nodded and Tyson kneeled down next to him.

Tyson liked to think of himself as being quite strong. He was the only one of his friends that could swing from one end of the monkey bars in the park and back again without putting his feet on the ground. He could also do five and a half press-ups without falling flat on his face and once beat his older cousin Ryan in an arm wrestle. Moving an old man, even a particularly tall one, shouldn't be a problem.

Tyson tried lifting the old man under his arms but couldn't even move him a centimetre. Then he tried pulling him from the front by his arms and even dug his heels into the lawn, but after a few tries the old man hadn't moved a bit and Tyson was afraid that if he carried on he might pull his arms right off. Finally Tyson told the old man that he was going to have to help too. 'You can't just lie there,' he explained. 'You have to help me help you.'

Tyson got the old man to put his hands flat on the ground and counted down from three to one and then yelled an almighty: 'Push!' The old man pushed, as Tyson braced himself and lifted. On the first try nothing happened, but on the second and third tries Tyson could feel the old man moving upwards, and within a few moments the old man was on his knees and in a much better position to get upright. They both fell silent for a moment, breathing hard with the exertion, then straining for all he was worth, Tyson gave the man one last tug.

'I did it!' yelled Tyson as the old man tottered upright before losing his balance and leaning so much of his body weight onto Tyson's shoulders that for a moment Tyson thought he might collapse. Tyson braced himself, though, and pushed against him until the old man finally regained his balance.

The old man was red in the face and didn't once look at Tyson as he dried his eyes and wiped his nose on the back of one of his huge, hairy hands. Tyson wondered if the old man was embarrassed and concluded that he probably was. Once Tyson skidded on some wet leaves when he and his friends were playing Bulldog in the park. As he lay on the ground they all laughed at him, even Ajay, and although he'd twisted his ankle, what hurt most was his pride. It doesn't really matter how old you are, thought Tyson as he walked the old man to his front door, no one likes being embarrassed when they fall over.

In the hallway of the man's house was a battered wooden dining chair that creaked loudly when the old man flopped down on it.

He looked at Tyson. 'Do you want money?'

Tyson shook his head. 'I'd better go.'

The old man nodded but then his eyes went moist again and he had to wipe them with his sleeve.

'There was some litter on the lawn,' said the old man, 'a crisp packet. She loved that lawn. It was her pride and joy.'

Tyson didn't know what the old man was talking about but reasoned that this wasn't a moment to ask questions.

'I'll see you around,' said Tyson, feeling like that was a good way to end the conversation.

Sitting on his bike outside the old man's house Tyson tried to make up his mind what to do: carry on to Ajay's even though they'd only have a short time to play or return home and tell his mum about what had happened? There was no contest: it had to be Ajay's.

Dodging imaginary bullets and explosions along with real-world chip wrappers and half-crushed Coke cans, as he zoomed off to the end of the road Tyson was already embellishing his encounter with the old man for Ajay's consumption. The old man would be a giant and weigh as much as a car, and after Tyson had helped him, the old man would offer him a real sword, which he couldn't accept because his mum wouldn't like it. He knew Ajay wouldn't believe him, but that was sort of the point. Like all good superheroes he couldn't risk giving away his secret identity. From now on to most people he would carry on being ordinary, everyday Tyson, who loved fried egg and oven chips and playing out on his bike, but to those in peril he would be the Good Sandyman: rescuer of the helpless, defender of the weak and brilliant at being on his bicycle.

THE MĂRȚIȘOARE

J. L. HALL

'The rain,' Bogdan said. 'It's easing.'

Louise looked up at the beaten sky, its pewter shifting to silver. The dampness in the air was lifting; the sounds of their footsteps rang louder now. She heard blackbirds and robins singing again, at last.

They had come to the park to visit their *mărțișoare*, their Romanian harvest blessings for the first of March, to give thanks, and to plead for money for the forthcoming year. Each spring, Bogdan's mother, Anca, posted the trinkets from Transylvania to London to be worn on the breast of his wife and his sister for one week, then tied to a tree branch for luck. Today the mărțișoare were sodden; rain ran down their woven braids in rivulets. The scarlet-and-white twisted threads were suspended from a beech tree overlooking the pond and clung, drenched, together. Louise and Bogdan reached up through the leaves to touch them, flinching as the rainwater trickled up their sleeves.

There were four mărțișoare on the branch: one for each year that Louise and Bogdan had been together. Each year the mărțișoare had delivered their hopes; money had come without much hand-wringing and soothed any dry spells, filling any cracks. This last year had been different. They had been pitched again and again into uncertainty with work and with health and had reeled from one crisis to the next. Louise was sick of it, desperate for respite from the unending strain and for the release, the peace that some security would at last bring, the heavy sleep that would surely return. 'This will pass,' Bogdan had cajoled her, frequently, on wretched, exhausted mornings as they sat in bed. 'It will get better.'

A *mărțișor*, Anca had explained one spring when they had visited her, was a talisman. A countryside custom to bring luck and prosperity to cattle and crops and family. She had slid a *mărțișor* across the kitchen table to Louise, showing her the miniature wooden charm and the interwoven tassels: the red signified blood, the white, regeneration; bound together they would bring good fortune. Louise had pinned it to her top with a laugh, patting her mother-in-law's hands and promising to wear it for one week. She fiddled with its braids as Anca returned to the stovetop to finish cooking the *ciorbă* soup, and a distant freight train rumbled past the window. This small gift had filled her with hope.

Louise shook the water from her cuffs, keen to leave their weekly ritual and to return to the warmth of their flat. To be at home cocooned in low lamplight with the windows fogging and the water hissing in the radiator pipes as something, anything, mindlessly played on the television. Huddled together in solace.

'Look! You can see the snowdrops.' Bogdan stooped over the wet soil around a nearby cherry tree and grinned. He fingered the green shoots. 'It's nearly spring.' He rose and inspected the tips of the tree's branches. 'This will start to bud in another couple of weeks.' He pulled Louise to him and wrapped an arm around her. 'See? Think of the blossom.'

She could feel the warmth of his breath on her ear, the scratch of his beard on her temple. He squeezed her shoulder and she forced a smile. 'You're right. It's nearly spring.' She spoke brightly, aiming to convince him of her optimism. She lightened her step, and flicked her glance from left to right as they crossed the small bridge. It was flanked by the pond on one side and the pond's overflow, which tumbled underneath the bridge to create another pool. The ice that had coated the water last week, causing ducks and moorhens and coots to skitter, had melted. Louise gazed upwards: the Japanese maple that hung over them was bare, but its russet stems were studded by the nibs of future leaves. Life was returning.

They walked together in silence along the path, splashed by occasional drops from the chestnuts' boughs above them. The tarmac glistened after the rain and its ruts were filled with puddles that mirrored the sky, flashes of blue amongst the grey. Louise felt the heat of Bogdan's palm around hers. She was safe; she was secure. This had to be enough, this, now. It was only spring, the rest of the year lay ahead of them. Good fortune would come.

They rounded the corner, past some hawthorn bushes. 'Oh!' Louise pointed as a flicker of red and white in the leaves caught her eye. 'Someone else has left a *mărțișor*!' She touched its ribbons, and wondered who had tied it there, and what hopes they held. What wishes and pleas they had made for their lives. Louise smiled at him. 'It's not just us.'

'No,' he replied. 'It's never just us. There are always others.'

OUT OF THE FLESH

CHRISTOPHER BROOKMYRE

Restorative justice, they cry it. That's what happens when wee scrotes like you get sat doon wi' their victims, mano a mano, kinda like you and me are daein' the noo. It's a process of talking and understanding, as opposed tae a chance for the likes ay me tae batter your melt in for tryin' tae tan my hoose. The idea is that us victims can put a face tae the cheeky midden that wheeched wur stereos, and yous can see that the gear you're pochlin' actually belongs tae somebody. 'Cause you think it's a gemme, don't you? Just aboot no' gettin' caught, and anyway, the hooses are insured, so it's naebody's loss, right? So the aim is tae make you realise that it's folk you're stealin' fae, and that it does a lot mair damage than the price ay a glazier and a phone call tae Direct Line.

Aye. Restorative justice. Just a wee blether tae make us baith feel better, that's the theory. Except it normally happens efter the courts and the polis are through wi' their end, by mutual consent and under official supervision. Cannae really cry this mutual consent, no' wi' you tied tae that chair. But restorative justice is whit you're gaunny get.

Aye. You're shittin' your breeks 'cause you think I'm gaunny leather you afore the polis get here, then make up whatever story I like. Tempting, I'll grant you, but ultimately futile. See, the point aboot restorative justice is that it helps the baith ay us. Me batterin' your melt in isnae gaunny make you think you're a mug for tannin' hooses, is it? It's just gaunny make ye careful the next time, when ye come back wi' three chinas and a big chib.

Believe me, you're lucky a batterin's aw you're afraid of, ya wee nyaff. Whit I'm gaunny tell you is worth mair than anythin' you were hopin' tae get away wi' fae here, an' if you're smart, you'll realise what a big favour I'm daein' ye.

Are you sittin' uncomfortably? Then I'll begin.

See, I used tae be just like you. Surprised, are ye? Nearly as surprised as when you tried tae walk oot this living room and found yoursel wi' a rope roon ye. I've been around and about, son. I never came up the Clyde in a banana boat and I wasnae born sixty, either. Just like you, did I say? Naw. Much worse. By your age I'd done mair hooses than the census. This was in the days when they said you could leave your back door open, and tae be fair, you could, as long as you didnae mind me and ma brer Billy nippin' in and helpin' oursels tae whatever was on offer.

We werenae fae the village originally; we were fae the Soothside. Me and Billy hud tae move in wi' oor uncle when ma faither went inside. Two wee toerags, fifteen and fourteen, fae a tenement close tae rural gentility. It wasnae so much fish oot ay watter as piranhas in a paddlin' pool. Easy pickin's, ma boy, easy pickin's. Open doors, open windaes, open wallets. Course, the problem wi' bein' piranhas in a paddlin' pool is it's kinda obvious whodunnit. At the end of the feedin' frenzy, when the watter's aw red, naebody's pointin' any fingers at the nearest koi carp, know what I'm sayin'? But you'll know yoursel', when you're that age, it's practically impossible for the polis or the courts tae get a binding result, between the letter ay the law and the fly moves ye can pull. Didnae mean ye were immune fae a good leatherin' aff the boys in blue, right enough, roon the back ay the station, but that's how I know applied retribution's nae use as a disincentive. Efter a good kickin', me and Billy were even mair determined tae get it up them; just meant we'd try harder no tae get caught.

But then wan night, aboot October time, the sergeant fronts up while me and Billy are kickin' a baw aboot. Sergeant, no less. Royalty. Gold-plated boot in the baws comin' up, we think. But naw, instead he's aw nicey-nicey, handin' oot fags, but keepin' an eye over his shoulder, like he doesnae want seen.

And by God, he doesnae. Fly bastard's playin' an angle, bent as a nine-bob note.

'I ken the score, boys,' he says. 'What's bred in the bone will not out of the flesh. Thievin's in your nature: I cannae change that, your uncle cannae change that, and when yous are auld enough, the jail willnae change that. So we baith might as well accept the situation and make the best ay it.'

'Whit dae ye mean?' I asks.

'I've a wee job for yous. Or mair like a big job, something tae keep ye in sweeties for a wee while so's ye can leave folk's hooses alane. Eejits like you are liable tae spend forever daein' the same penny-ante shite, when there's bigger prizes on offer if you know where tae look.'

Then he lays it aw doon, bold as brass. There's a big hoose, a mansion really, a couple ay miles ootside the village. Me and Billy never knew it was there; well, we'd seen the gates, but we hadnae thought aboot what was behind them, 'cause you couldnae see anythin' for aw the trees. The owner's away in London, he says, so the housekeeper and her husband are bidin' in tae keep an eye on the place. But the sergeant's got the inside gen that the pair ay them are goin' tae some big

Halloween party in the village. Hauf the toon's goin', in fact, includin' him, which is a handy wee alibi for while we're daein' his bidding.

There was ayeways a lot o' gatherings among the in-crowd in the village, ma uncle tell't us. Shady affairs, he said. Secretive, like. He reckoned they were up tae all sorts, ye know? Wife-swappin' or somethin'. Aw respectable on the ootside, but a different story behind closed doors. Course, he would say that, seein' as the crabbit auld bugger never got invited.

Anyway, the sergeant basically tells us it's gaunny be carte blanche. This was the days before fancy burglar alarms an' aw that shite, remember, so we'd nothin' tae worry aboot regards security. But he did insist on somethin' a bit strange, which he said was for all of oor protection: we'd tae 'make it look professional, but no' too professional'. We understood what he meant by professional: don't wreck the joint or dae anythin' that makes it obvious whodunnit. But the 'too professional' part was mair tricky, it bein' aboot disguisin' the fact it was a sortay inside job.

'Whit ye oan aboot?' I asked him. 'Whit's too professional? Polishin' his flair and giein' the woodwork a dust afore we leave?'

'I'm talkin' aboot bein' canny whit you steal. The man's got things even an accomplished burglar wouldnae know were worth a rat's fart – things only valuable among collectors, so you couldnae fence them anyway. I don't want you eejits knockin' them by mistake, cause it'll point the finger back intae the village. If you take them, he'll know the thief had prior knowledge, as opposed tae just hittin' the place because it's a country mansion.'

'So whit are these things?'

'The man's a magician – on the stage, like. That's what he's daein' doon in London. He's in variety in wan o' thae big West

End theatres. But that's just showbusiness, how he makes his money. The word is, he's intae some queer, queer stuff, tae dae wi' the occult.'

'Like black magic?'

'Aye. The man's got whit ye cry "artefacts". Noo I'm no' sayin' ye'd be naturally inclined tae lift them, and I'm no' sure you'll even come across them, 'cause I don't know where they're kept, but I'm just warnin' you tae ignore them if ye dae. Take cash, take gold, take jewels, just the usual stuff − and leave anythin' else well enough alone.'

'Got ye.'

'And wan last thing, boys: if you get caught, this conversation never took place. Naebody'd believe your word against mine anyway.'

So there we are. The inside nod on a serious score and a guarantee fae the polis that it's no' gaunny be efficiently investigated. Sounded mair like Christmas than Halloween, but it pays tae stay a wee bit wary, especially wi' the filth involved − and bent filth at that, so we decided tae ca' canny.

Come the big night, we took the wise precaution of takin' a train oot the village and, mair importantly, made sure we were seen takin' it by the station staff. The two piranha had tae be witnessed gettin' oot the paddlin' pool, for oor ain protection. We bought return tickets tae Glesca Central, but got aff at the first stop, by which time the inspector had got a good, alibi-corroboratin' look at us. We'd planked two stolen bikes behind a hedge aff the main road earlier in the day, and cycled our way back, lyin' oot flat at the side ay the road the odd time a motor passed us.

It took longer than we thought, mainly because it was awfy dark and you cannae cycle very fast when you cannae see where you're goin'. We liked the dark, me and Billy. It suited us, felt natural tae us, you know? But that night just seemed thon wee bit blacker than usual, maybe because we were oot in the countryside. It was thon wee bit quieter as well, mair still, which should have made us feel we were alone tae oor ain devices, but I couldnae say that was the case. Instead it made me feel kinda exposed, like I was a wee moose and some big owl was gaunny swoop doon wi' nae warnin' and huckle us away for its tea.

And that was before we got tae the hoose.

'Bigger prizes,' we kept sayin' tae each other. 'Easy money.' But it didnae feel like easy anythin' efter we'd climbed over the gates and started walkin' up that path, believe me. If we thought it was dark on the road, that was nothin' compared tae in among thae tall trees. Then we saw the hoose. Creepy as, I'm tellin' you. Looked twice the size it would have in daylight, I'm sure, high and craggy, towerin' above like it was leanin' over tae check us oot. Dark stone, black glass reflectin' fuck-all, and on the top floor a light on in wan wee windae.

'There's somebody in, Rab,' Billy says. 'The game's a bogey. Let's go hame.'

Which was a very tempting notion, I'll admit, but no' as tempting as playin' pick and mix in a mansion full o' goodies.

'Don't be a numpty,' I says. 'They've just left a light on by mistake. As if there wouldnae be lights on doonstairs if somebody was hame. C'mon.'

'Aye, aw right,' Billy says, and we press on.

We make oor way roon the back, lookin' for a likely wee windae. Force of habit, goin' roon the back, forgettin' there's naebody tae see us if we panned in wan o' the ten-footers at the front. I'm cuttin' aboot lookin' for a good-sized stane tae brek the glass, when Billy reverts tae the mair basic technique of just tryin' the back door, which swings open easy as you like. Efter that, it's through and intae the kitchen, where we find some candles and matches. Billy's aw for just stickin' the lights on as we go, but I'm still no' sure that sneaky bastard sergeant isnae gaunny come breengin' in wi' a dozen polis any minute, so I'm playin' it smart.

Oot intae the hallway and I'm soon thinkin', *Knackers tae smart, let there be light.* The walls just disappear up intae blackness; I mean, there had tae be a ceiling up there somewhere, but Christ knows how high. Every footstep's echoin' roon the place, every breath's bein' amplified like I'm walkin' aboot inside ma ain heid. But maistly it was the shadows … Aw, man, the shadows. I think fae that night on, I'd rather be in the dark than in candlelight, that's whit the shadows were daein' tae me. And aw the time, of course, it's gaun through my mind, the sergeant's words … *queer, stuff … the occult.* Black magic. Doesnae help that it's Halloween, either, every bugger tellin' stories aboot ghosts and witches aw week.

But I tell myself: *Screw the nut, got a job tae dae here. Get on, get oot, and we'll be laughin' aboot this when we're sittin' on that last train hame fae Central.* So we get busy, start tannin' rooms. First couple are nae use. I mean, quality gear, but nae use tae embdy withoot a furniture lorry. Big paintin's and statues and the like. Then third time lucky: intae this big room wi' aw these display cabinets. A lot ay it's crystal and china – again, nae use, but we can see the sergeant wasnae haverin'. There's jewellery, ornaments: plenty of gold and silver and nae shortage of gemstones embedded either.

'If it sparkles, bag it,' I'm tellin' Billy, and we're laughin' away until we baith hear somethin'. It's wan o' thae noises you cannae quite place, cannae work oot exactly whit it sounded like or where it was comin' fae, but you know you heard it: deep, rumbling and low.

'Whit was that?'

'You heard it an' aw?'

'Aye. Ach, probably just the wind,' I says, no even kiddin' masel.

'Was it fuck the wind. It sounded like a whole load ay people singin' or somethin'.'

'Well, I cannae hear it noo, so never bother.'

'Whit aboot that light? Whit if somebody is up there?'

'It didnae sound like it came fae above. Maist likely the plumbing. The pipes in these big auld places can make some weird sounds.'

Billy doesnae look sure, but he gets on wi' his job aw the same.

We go back tae the big hallway, but stop and look at each other at the foot of the stairs. We baith know what the other's thinkin': there's mair gear tae be had up there, but neither ay us is in a hurry to go lookin' for it. That said, there's still room in the bags, and I'm about to suggest we grasp the thistle when we hear the rumblin' sound again. *Could be the pipes*, I'm thinkin', but I know what Billy meant when he said lots ay folk singin'.

'We're no' finished doon here,' I says, postponin' the issue a wee bit, and we go through another door aff the hall. It's a small room, compared to the others anyway, and the curtains are shut, so I reckon it's safe to stick the light on. The light seems dazzling at first, but that's just because we'd become accustomed tae the dark. It's actually quite low, cannae be mair than forty watt. The room's an office, like, a study. There's a big desk in the middle, a fireplace on wan wall and bookshelves aw the way tae the ceiling, apart fae where the windae is.

Billy pulls a book aff the shelf, big ancient-lookin' leather-bound effort. 'Have a swatch at this,' he says, pointin' tae the open page. 'Diddies! Look.'

He's right. There's a picture ay a wummin in the scud lyin' doon oan a table; no' a photie, like, a drawin', an' aw this queer writin' underneath, in letters I don't recognise. *Queer, queer stuff*, I remember. *Occult. Black magic.*

Billy turns the page. 'Euuh!'

There's a picture ay the same wummin, but there's a boay in a long robe plungin' her wi' a blade.

'Put it doon,' I says, and take the book aff him.

But it's no' just books that's on the shelves. There's aw sorts o' spooky-lookin' gear. Wee statues, carved oot ay wood. Wee women wi' big diddies, wee men wi' big boabbies. Normally we'd be pishin' oorsels at these, but there's somethin' giein' us the chills aboot this whole shebang. There's masks as well, some of wood, primitive efforts, but some others in porcelain or alabaster: perfect likenesses of faces, but solemn, grim even. I realise they're death masks, but don't say anythin' tae Billy.

'These must be thon arty hingmies the sergeant warned us aboot,' Billy says. 'Artefacts. Aye. I'm happy tae gie them a bodyswerve. Let's check the desk and that'll dae us.'

'Sure.'

We try the drawers on one side. They're locked, and we've no' brought anythin' tae jemmy them open.

'Forget it,' I say, hardly able tae take my eyes aff thae death masks, but Billy gie's the rest ay the drawers a pull just for the sake ay it. The bottom yin rolls open, a big, deep, heavy thing.

'Aw, man,' Billy says.

The drawer contains a glass case, and inside ay it is a skull, restin' on a bed ay velvet. 'Dae ye think it's real?' Billy asks.

'Oh Christ aye,' I says. I've never seen a real skull, except in photies, so I wouldnae know, but I'd put money on it aw the same. I feel weird: it's giein' me the chills but I'm drawn tae it at the same time. I want tae touch it. I put my hands in and pull at the glass cover, which lifts aff, nae bother.

'We cannae take it, Rab,' Billy says. 'Mind whit the sergeant tell't us.'

'I just want tae haud it,' I tell him. I reach in and take haud ay it carefully with both hands, but it doesnae lift away. It's like it's connected tae somethin' underneath, but I can tell there's some give in it, so I try giein' it a wee twist. It turns aboot ninety degrees, courtesy of a flick o' the wrist, at which point the pair ay us nearly hit the ceilin', 'cause there's a grindin' noise at oor backs and we turn roon tae see that the back ay the fireplace has rolled away.

'It's a secret passage,' Billy says. 'I read aboot these. Big auld hooses hud them fae back in the times when they might get invaded.'

I look into the passage, expecting darkness, but see a flickerin' light, dancin' aboot like it must be comin' fae a fire. Me and Billy looks at each other. We baith know we're shitin' oorsels, but we baith know there's no way we're no' checkin' oot whatever's doon this passage.

We leave the candles because there's just aboot enough light, and we don't want tae gie oorsels away too soon if it turns oot there's somebody doon there. I go first. I duck doon tae get under the mantelpiece, but the passage is big enough for us tae staun upright once I'm on the other side. It only goes three or four yards and then there's a staircase, a tight spiral number. I haud on tae the walls as I go doon, so's my footsteps are light and quiet. I stop haufway doon and put a hand oot tae stop Billy an' aw, because we can hear a voice. It's a man talkin', except it's almost like he's singin', like a priest giein' it that high-and-mighty patter. Then we hear that sound again, and Billy was right: it is loads ay people aw at once, chantin' a reply tae whatever the man's said.

Queer, queer stuff, I'm thinkin'. *Occult. Black magic.*

Still, I find masel creepin' doon the rest ay the stairs. I move slow as death as I get to the bottom, and crouch in close tae the wall tae stay oot ay sight. Naebody sees us, 'cause they're aw facin' forwards away fae us in this long underground hall, kinda like a chapel but wi' nae windaes. It's lit wi' burnin' torches alang baith walls, a stone table – I suppose you'd cry it an altar – at the far end, wi' wan o' yon pentagrams painted on the wall behind it. There's aboot two dozen folk, aw wearin' these big black hooded robes, except for two ay them at the altar: the bloke that's giein' it the priest patter, who's in red, and a lassie, no' much aulder than us, in white, wi' a gag roon her mooth. She looks dazed, totally oot ay it. Billy crouches doon next tae us. We don't look at each other 'cause we cannae take oor eyes aff what's happenin' at the front.

The boy in the red robe, who must be the magician that owns the joint, gie's a nod, and two of the congregation come forward and lift the lassie. It's only when they dae this that I can see her hands are tied behind her back and her feet are tied together at her ankles. They place her doon on the altar and then drape a big white sheet over her, coverin' her fae heid tae toe. Then the boy in red starts chantin' again, and pulls this huge dagger oot fae his robe. He hauds it above his heid, and everythin' goes totally still, totally quiet. Ye can hear the cracklin' ay the flames aw roon the hall. Then the congregation come oot wi' that rumblin' chant again, and he plunges the dagger doon intae the sheet.

There's mair silence, and I feel like time's staunin' still for a moment; like when it starts again this'll no' be true. Then I see the red startin' tae seep across the white sheet, and a second later it's drippin' aff the altar ontae the flair.

'Aw Jesus,' I says. I hears masel sayin' it afore I know whit I'm daein', an' by that time it's too late.

Me and Billy turns and scrambles back up the stair as fast as, but when we get tae the top, it's just blackness we can see. The fireplace has closed over again. We see the orange flickerin' ay torches and hear footsteps comin' up the stairs, the two ay us slumped doon against a wall, haudin' on tae each other. Two men approach, then stop a few feet away, which is when wan ay them pulls his hood back.

'Evening, boys. We've been expecting you,' he says. The fuckin' sergeant.

'I assume you took steps to make sure nobody knew where you were going tonight,' he goes on. I remember the train, the guard, the bikes, the return ticket in my trooser pocket. The sergeant smiles. 'Knew you wouldn't let us down. What's bred in the bone will not out of the flesh.'

Four more blokes come up tae lend a hand. They tie oor hauns and feet, same as the lassie, and huckle us back doon the stair tae the hall.

'Two more sacrifices, Master,' the sergeant shouts oot tae the boy in red. 'As promised.'

'Are they virgins?' the Master says.

'Come on. Would anybody shag this pair?'

The Master laughs and says: 'Bring them forward.'

We get carried, lyin' on oor backs, by two guys each, and it's as we pass down the centre of the hall that we see the faces peerin' in. It's aw folk fae the village. Folk we know, folk we've stolen from. I think aboot ma uncle and his blethers aboot secret gatherings. Auld bastard never knew the hauf ay it.

'This one first,' the Master says, and they lie me doon on the altar, which is still damp wi' blood. I feel it soakin' intae ma troosers as the boy starts chantin' again and a fresh white sheet comes doon tae cover me.

I don't know whether there was ether on it, or chloroform,

or maybe it was just fear, but that was the last thing I saw, 'cause I passed oot aboot two seconds later.

So.

Ye don't need many brains tae work oot what happened next, dae ye? Aye, a lesson was taught. A wise and skilled man, that magician, for he was the man in charge, the village in his thrall, willingly daein' what he told them.

Suffice it to say, that was two wee scrotes who never broke intae another hoose, and the same'll be true of you, pal.

I can see fae that look in your eye that you're sceptical aboot this. Maybe you don't believe you're no' gaunny reoffend. Nae changin' your nature, eh? What's bred in the bone will not out of the flesh. Or maybe you don't believe my story?

Aye, that's a fair shout. I didnae tell the whole truth. The story's nae lie, but I changed the perspective a wee bit, for dramatic effect. You see, if you werenae so blissfully oblivious of whose hoose you happen tae be screwin' on any given night, you might have noticed fae the doorplate that my name's no Rab. I wasnae wan ay the burglars.

I was the sergeant.

I'm retired noo, obviously, but I still perform certain services in the village. We're a close-knit community, ye could say. So I ought to let you know, when you heard me on the phone earlier, sayin' I'd caught a burglar and tae come roon soon as, it wasnae 999 I dialled. Mair like 666, if you catch my drift. 'Cause, let's face it, naebody knows you're here, dae they?

Are you a virgin, by the way? Aye, right.

Doesnae matter, really. Either way, you're well fucked noo.

Aye, good evening, officer, thanks for coming. He's through there. Sorry aboot the whiff. I think you could call that the smell of restorative justice.

Go easy on him. I've a strong feelin' he's aboot tae change his ways. A magical transformation, you could cry it.

How do I know? Personal experience, officer. Personal experience.

SINGLE SPEED

JOEL BLACKLEDGE

For Christmas, Dad got me a bicycle. Flat-bar hybrid, single speed, carbon fork, aluminium frame, ergonomic grips, 29er wheels. Second-hand – no doubt about it – but clean, sturdy, and light enough to lift with one hand. He said it's for when the fascists take over.

The bike was leaning against the tree, a red bow between the handlebars. Dad presented it with a 'ta-da!' when I came downstairs, then took the bow off and started tinkering with it.

'Bikes don't need more than one gear, pet,' he said with his face against the frame, 'and anyone who says otherwise is afraid of hard work.'

My dad says that Mussolini never actually made the trains run on time. He says it's a myth invented by fascist apologists so that everyone, even normally sensible people, would always have a good word to say about Mussolini. Public transport in fascist Italy was just as messy as the rest of the state, so Italian anti-fascists would have used bikes. In a tight spot, my dad says, you appreciate a light bike.

Last Christmas he gave me a T-shirt that read 'THIS DAUGHTER KILLS FASCISTS' and made me wear it to school for the first day back. Danny Palmer from my class saw it and asked the teacher what a fascist is and I had to go to the deputy head's office. Now I only wear the T-shirt to sleep in.

Granddad got me a book about the Battle of Cable Street. It was an oral history book, and he was even in it – though I had heard his Cable Street stories so often that I could have written that part myself. It was his favourite thing to talk about: how he marched down the middle of the road arm in arm with a trade unionist and a rabbi, singing 'The Internationale' while housewives came tearing down into the street, rolling pins in hand, to join the procession. He'd taken out three fascists himself before he was beaten back by the police.

'It's the duty of the young,' he would say, pointing a bony finger at me and sloshing tea around his mug.

The fact that he was only six years old at the time wasn't mentioned in the book.

Ted came down to the living room, wearing his Woody Guthrie jumper that he only got out for special occasions. Ted's my big brother. His present from Dad was an old-fashioned shaving kit, with a straight cutthroat razor and leather case. Ted loved it, even though I knew he was trying to grow a beard.

We swapped presents. I got him one of those little machines that rolls your cigarettes for you.

'But Rosa,' he said, turning the machine's handle sceptically, 'I can roll my own smokes.'

He'd started smoking roll-ups a few months before and I felt bad that they kept falling apart in his mouth. I could roll better than him and I wasn't even old enough to buy tobacco. I told him that if it really bothered him he could pre-roll a load before he goes out. And who calls them *smokes*, anyway?

He passed me a square present wrapped in a copy of the *Morning Star*. I ripped straight through the headline and uncovered the doughy face of General Franco, wearing a big fur collar and lit like an old Hollywood movie star.

'It's a book about the Spanish Civil War,' he said, his cigarette burning up in a big orange flame that almost touched his fringe. 'All the stuff that Great-Granddad Peter did.'

Granddad gave a solemn slurp of his tea at the mention of his father, who had spent half a year in Catalonia with an anarchist militia. Him and Dad talked about it all the time. They talked less about the Spanish woman who phoned last year claiming to be from Peter's second family.

I flicked through the photos in the middle of the book. There were some more of Franco, as well as some of women in military uniform leaning on sandbags and smiling for the camera.

'Hey, did you know that Franco's nickname was Miss Canary Islands 1936?' Ted was nodding as he inhaled, stifling a cough. 'He stayed there instead of joining in with the war, the coward.'

'Can't say I blame him,' I said quietly.

Granddad was opening his present from me: some *Buffy* DVDs, because despite being almost ninety years old, and having eyes, he'd never seen it. He held it at arm's length and squinted, making sense of it.

'Oh, American, is it?' he said, putting the DVDs to one side to use as a coaster.

Dad was tearing the paper off the present I got him. He held it in both hands and let out a low, breathy chuckle.

'Oh, Rosa, that's great, that! That's champion!'

It was an almanac for FC St Pauli, who are my dad's favourite football club even though St Pauli are from Hamburg and he's from Gateshead. But they are an anti-fascist club, so they're his team. The almanac had all the team's statistics for the previous thirty years, as well as a short history of how they were founded and interviews with current and past players. My dad was flicking through it, beaming.

'Oh, it's just champion!'

I immediately regretted the gift. I knew that he would construe it as some sort of expression of interest in football on my part. I'd been to a match once, when Dad took us on holiday to Hamburg. There was a big group of men there who all knew Dad, and they drank so much beer during the game that by the end I didn't even know what they were shouting for. One man with a thick walrus moustache could barely speak a word of English but he wanted to show off for me and so he kept shouting, 'Victory is likely!' and elbowing me in the ribs.

My dad gave a constant commentary. Everything the team did was 'very smart' or a 'bold move' or just 'champion', even when they were three-nil down. He'd tap my shoulder and point out a formation, explain how they played like no one else, how they based their tactics on solidarity. I couldn't see the pitch over all the cheering men, but even if I could, I wouldn't be interested. I mean, how revolutionary can kicking a ball really be? You either get it in the goal or you don't – and mostly they didn't.

Dad brought the almanac over to me and we looked through it together. It was full of all the information he had already told me about the club.

'We'll have a look at their fixtures, find another match we can go to.' His eyes were glued to the book. 'Hey, it could be your birthday present!'

'Why don't we take the bike out?' I said, standing up.

It was warm for Christmas Day. The streets were empty and the sun was out, though I could see my breath. We were going to take the bike to the park, but as there was no traffic, we just stayed in our street.

'Look at this,' said my dad, extending his arms out to the quiet, wet street, 'one holy baby and the whole country stands still. You couldn't imagine this sort of mobilisation for a barricade, could you? I tell you, this is why the fascists are going to take over.'

I'm not sure people staying at home for a day counted as mobilisation, but I let him go on.

'That's the idea behind the bike, pet,' he said, patting the seat. 'You see how easy it is to shut things down? No public transport, no infrastructure, no nothing. Services are run by people, and people scare easy. With a bike, you can get around the roadblocks and all that. You can help people. Warn people. Like Paul Revere on his horse. Except, you know, on a bike.'

'Yeah, thanks, Dad,' I said, climbing onto the saddle. 'Hey, maybe tomorrow we can all go and see the new *Mission: Impossible* film?'

'Why, who's in it?'

I shrugged. 'Tom Cruise, probably.'

'He's a bit of a loon, isn't he? And there's that pub quiz tomorrow – legal costs fundraiser.'

'Yeah,' I said, and I pedalled away down the middle of the street. The bike responded to my every move, turning at the slightest bend of my hips. The clack of the spokes, the soft hush of the rubber, the cold air teasing my skin. A simple twist and I'm away where I want, away where none can follow.

At end of the road I found Danny Palmer from school. He was alone and looking up at the sky.

'All right, Danny? Merry Christmas,' I said, pulling up next to him.

'All right, Rosa,' he replied, casting a quick glance my way.

Above us, a small white drone was flying up and down, sending out a high-pitched buzzing that echoed all down the street. In Danny's hands was a chunky remote control that he was tentatively nudging with both thumbs.

'Is that your Christmas present, then?' I asked.

'That's right,' he sniffed. 'What about you?'

'Dad got me this bike,' I said.

He looked once at the bike and gave a grunt. The drone continued its up-down motion.

'What can you do with that, then?' I asked.

Danny shrugged and flew the drone around in a circle.

I climbed onto the bike and cycled away, back down the road. Through front windows I saw other families having their own Christmas mornings – faces turned inward to each other, deaf to the sounds of the street below. I finally reached my dad and he gave another low chuckle.

'How's it ride, pet?'

'Champion,' I said, and we went back inside for a cup of tea. Poor Danny Palmer. He won't stand a chance when the fascists take over.

THE DISH WITH THE DANCING COWS

MEERA SYAL

It started with a leak. A crack in the guttering between our two flats. So every time it rained, which was a lot lately – 'Global warming, see?' my mum had said, always the voice of doom when a rain shower suddenly became the end of the world – we'd hear it. Drip drip drip. Right outside our kitchen window. Especially loud when we would sit in silence at our tiny table, just big enough for me, Mum and Taz, my little bro, and the noise of the dripping water became as loud as a drum. A sad, watery drum, thumping away like a reluctant heartbeat, marking each moment that Dad was missing, reminding us how much we were missing him.

'Like bloomin' Chinese water torture,' Mum had grumbled as she mopped up the little pool of water that would collect just outside our front door after a particularly heavy downfall.

'That's racist!' Taz shouted, looking up from his library book. Yep, he read books. He actually prefers them to iPads. Not that he had one, but if he had one, he'd still have his head in a Harry Potter or a Malorie Blackman. Weird kid, I know. Doesn't say much, but when he does it's usually shouty and to the point.

'Don't be daft!' Mum said back. 'I'm a half-Hindu, half-Catholic Mancunian. I married an African Muslim and I gave away most of my bingo wins to Comic Relief last time. One thing I'm not is racist.'

And then, especially loudly by the open kitchen window, she boomed, 'Yup, I think you'll find I'm not the Racist One Around Here!'

And she smiled contentedly when in response, she heard the loud bang next door of exactly the same kitchen window being slammed shut.

So the puddle of water outside our front door never quite went. Because Mum would only ever clean up half the puddle. Her half. The other half was next door's problem. In fact, the leak itself was next door's problem. Mum proved it one day by getting out an actual tape measure and marching us both out to the balcony, where she proceeded to mark a straight line with the ribbon of wobbly steel from the leaky gutter to the floor, marking where it landed with a piece of chalk she'd nicked from Taz's craft box.

'See!' she crowed triumphantly. 'It's on her side. She's got to fix it. Let her spend three hours on the phone to the council. No skin off my banana, innit?'

Taz winced at Mum's attempt at down-with-the-kidz street talk. I was wincing for entirely different reasons. The chalk line didn't prove anything: how could you tell exactly where the crack was? What mattered was where the water fell, and it fell outside both our front doors. I also wondered how we looked, the three of us, standing outside our flat. Rows of front doors just like ours on every balcony, twelve floors, each balcony facing the centre so we could all see everyone's comings and goings from our kitchen windows. Probably the architect who designed this place reckoned this would be a good thing, it would encourage neighbourly feelings, people waving hello at each other across the divides, calling each other in for a cuppa and a natter. It also meant everyone in the block could see the angry woman in her faded dressing gown shouting at a gutter, the small bespectacled boy next to her humming tunelessly to himself to block out the shouting and the awkward lanky teenage girl between them, wishing to God she was somewhere else, hoping that whoever saw them might know what had happened to us, and see that her mum wasn't mad, just very very sad.

Our next-door neighbour was called Mrs Daniels. She was ancient. She never went out. She had a Tesco delivery once a week, mainly cans of stuff, long-life milk and biscuits. And she banged on the wall. A lot. Firstly it was because of our TV noise, Taz always turned it up extra loud whenever anything with David Attenborough was on, same with Mum with *First Dates* and Dad with cricket. We soon stopped doing that.

'She's old,' my dad told us. 'We were brought up to respect our elders. And she's on her own. So let's be kind.'

So we were. And we were the same with any music we played, or any friends we had round, which wasn't often, because me and Taz shared a room, so hanging out with our homies was done either in the sitting room/kitchen, with Mum trying to join in with our conversations – 'I love rap, me. That Jay-Cee's very good, isn't he?' – or in our shared bedroom with everyone squashed onto one of the bunk beds, top bunk for my mates, bottom for Taz's. But even on those rare occasions, one raised voice, one squeal of excitement, one peal of laughter and Mrs Daniels' banging would start. Boom boom on the sitting-room wall until we piped down. Dad went round once to try and have a relaxed chat about the banging, but even he didn't get past Mrs Daniels' front door. 'She shouted at me through the letterbox. Sounds like she's got fifty deadbolts on that door.'

'Shame she ain't got one on her mouth. Or her bloomin' stick,' muttered Mum.

'Ah, Mimi,' Dad chuckled, pulling Mum to him, 'Always the firecracker, never the water. Where's your water? Flow, be calm, water will always find its way.'

Dad said a lot of this sort of stuff: quick-fix spiritual nuggets, the kind you'd find on calendars or postcards stuck on people's computers. But coming from him, they would always sound like common sense. Or maybe that's just my memory making him better and more perfect than he was. Ironic that he wasn't around to deal with the actual water when it arrived.

On the day It happened, he'd pushed a note through Mrs Daniels' door. 'One last try,' he'd joked with Mum before he set off to work.

'You haven't used one of my best notelets, have you?' Mum had yelled at him as he stood on the balcony, licking the envelope shut before pushing it through Mrs Daniels' rusting letterbox.

'No, course not!'

He had winked at me, hoisted his rucksack on his back and waved as he took to the stairs. Always took the stairs, hated lifts – brought back too many memories, of hiding in cupboards and under beds as men with guns rampaged through his home, of being hidden in trucks and carts under tarpaulin and blankets, struggling to breathe and stay quiet at the same time, of being counted and labelled and box-ticked and spat at and dumped and finally delivered like an out-of-date, unwanted parcel; so many layers of confinement, darkness and fear rippled into his blood and bones. So he never took the lift. Or the Underground.

I wish I could say there was some special moment between us during that last minute with him, some long, significant look of tenderness and pride, a look that told me how proud he was of me, how he was so glad I was his daughter, of how amazing it was that somehow he and Mum had beaten lottery odds to find each other across oceans and borders, over mountains of family prejudice and disapproval, and find love and make me and Taz, and find a home and happiness. But he just winked, that was it, and he was gone, never to return.

The day of his funeral was the day Mum declared war on Mrs Daniels. Our little flat was full of wailing women with Mum sitting in the centre of them, completely silent and dry-eyed, the still centre of this tornado of grief, made worse by how stupid it all was, that a man who had survived the unspeakable should be knocked off his bike and killed by a number 27 bus. What made it even weirder was that fact both my grandmas were there, 'The Hindu one and the Muslim one. Both in the same room,' Taz had breathed as the two old ladies glared at each other from opposite sofas in between their competitive crying bouts, as if whoever cried the loudest would feel less guilty about never wanting Mum and Dad to marry in the first place.

And in the middle of all this, the banging started from next door. Thump thump on the wall, louder and angrier than we'd ever had it before. The grandmas tried to ignore it and redoubled their wailing efforts; for a while it was like some weird world-music mash-up, ancient primal ululations with a cockney dub beat underneath. And then Mum stood up and threw herself at the wall, banging it with her fists again and again, screaming, 'Shut up! Shut up, you old bag! My husband's dead! He's dead! He's dead!' and when the grandmas finally joined forces to pull Mum away, she had left a trail of bloody handprints that we could never quite scrub away afterwards.

So, six months on, the leak started it all up again. And this time we didn't have Dad to be UN peacekeeper, so me and Taz were on edge all the time, waiting for the next stage in border escalations. Until the day the dripping stopped. One minute we were sitting at the kitchen table, me and Taz desperately trying to keep talking to fill any silence in which Mum might hone in on the splish-splash outside, and then suddenly, it was gone. We all held our breath and cocked our ears, honestly like a row of spaniels, heads on one side, alert. No, definitely, it had stopped. Without speaking, we all flung ourselves onto the balcony and there, under the guttering, on the floor in between our two kitchen doors, was a large china dish decorated with a pattern of cows. Smiling, very English, brown glossy cows, each with a daisy in their mouths, caught in mid-skip as they danced their way around the sides in a bovine conga line. The splish-splash was now a gentle plip-plop; the floor was dry: it was, as we all knew, a gesture of peace of some kind. Mum sniffed and drew her dressing gown tight around herself. She had hardly been out of it since Dad's funeral and it was now stained with dried food and smelt like an old cat, but she never took it off long enough for us to sneak it into the wash.

'Nasty dish,' she said, and went back inside.

'So what happens when the dish gets full?' Taz whispered to me as we watched Mum gather up the breakfast plates. We were whispering because this was the first time Mum had actually tidied up for ages and we didn't want to break the momentum. We'd got used to clearing up after her; she'd leave anything she'd used behind her like a snail trail – cups, tissues, towels, even nail clippings. This from a woman who was so fanatically house-proud that she'd use the Dustbuster to pick up crumbs as we were eating toast – actually as we were eating it – hoovering our laps as we struggled to swallow. Well annoying. So watching her washing up was weirdly comforting.

'When the dish gets full,' I whispered back, 'we empty it and put it back.'

'Behind Mum's back?'

'Desperate times require desperate measures,' I recited.

'Like lying?'

'Yup. Until Mum's better.'

A pause. Taz chewed a fingernail thoughtfully. 'What if she doesn't get better?'

'She will,' I said, like a liar.

However, we didn't need to empty the dish with the dancing cows because a couple of weeks later, just as the water level of the dish was reaching its lip – because of course me and Taz had been checking it every day – two men in donkey jackets arrived with ladders and holdalls and set up outside our kitchen window.

Mum shot out of the bedroom with impressive speed and yanked up the net curtain. 'Who are they? What are they doing?'

I made for the front door, but Mum pulled me back. Her hand on my arm was as thin and strong as a claw.

'No – might be her next door up to something. You stay here. I'll go.'

She took a step, then suddenly looked down at herself, surprised. She took in the crusty dressing gown; she sniffed a sleeve and inhaled sharply.

'I stink. Why didn't you tell me? Tch.' And she stomped off to the bathroom. Ten minutes later she emerged in her favourite tracksuit, purple velour giving her the look of a fluffy aubergine, hair brushed and yes, I even saw a trace of lip gloss.

'Right,' she said, 'let's see what the old cow with the cow dish is up to, shall we?' and marched out onto the balcony. I only just stopped myself from giving her a round of applause. Taz and I watched from the window as Mum first glared, then harangued, then chatted, then smiled, then laughed with the men, then banged on the window and ordered us to make two cups of tea, milk, two sugars, and bring out the nice biscuits, and then, an hour later, after me and Taz had wandered off, bored, and how good that felt, to be bored rather than scared, Mum flung open the door and called, 'Hey! You two! Come and see!'

We stood next to Mum and gazed up at the guttering – a bright grey plastic section clearly stood out in the worn metal pipework – and nodded in what we hoped was a supportive way. Mum was flushed with excitement, bright-eyed as if she'd got up on the ladder and fixed it herself. It was all going well, Mum thanking the workmen, who seemed a bit embarrassed – maybe no one said thank you to them quite so often and loudly – until one of them held out towards Mum the dish with the dancing cows.

'What's this?'

'Your dish, Mrs Arif?'

'Not my dish!' Mum said deliberately loudly and went inside. The workman shrugged and handed the dish to me. I took it and followed Mum in. When she saw me holding it, she went ballistic.

'Why! Why did you do that, Serena?'

'Do what?'

'Take it! Take the dish?'

'Why not? It's not infected or anything, is it?'

Mum was starting at it maliciously, at me, all her good humour gone. I didn't know what I had done wrong.

'Now I will have to give it back to Her!'

'Well, I can do that if you don't want to—'

'Nooo! You don't understand! You don't.'

Mum slumped at the table, like someone had cut her strings.

She took a deep breath, and Taz and I exhaled with her. I know we both felt the black crows hovering at her shoulder, the darkness that had been shrouding Mum for so long flapping its wings ready to swoop and settle on her again. And we didn't want them back.

'You see,' she said, in a tired voice, 'when someone gives … lends you an empty dish, you can't send it back empty. It's not … right.'

'Who says?' Taz asked loudly, eyes shining as he sat next to Mum. He sniffed a story and we hadn't had one off Mum for a long time.

'It's a thing. A cultural thing. Not a religious thing,' she said quickly, sensing the question on Taz's lips. 'Maybe the only thing I was brought up with that I still believe. Not heaven. Not hell. They're both here, I know that now. But this one I sort of liked. If you borrow a dish from someone, you never give it back empty.'

'So what do you put in it?' Taz and I both asked the same question at the same time, which made a small smile flicker across Mum's face.

'Food,' she said. Her eyes softened as she continued, 'My mum was always borrowing bowls and dishes and Tupperware from her friends. Everybody always cooked too much because not having enough was the worst thing that could possibly happen if you were feeding guests in your home, so we all took leftovers back with us. That way nobody had to cook the next day. It was a bit annoying sometimes, seeing an ice-cream carton in the freezer and opening it expecting raspberry ripple and finding your Auntie Pinky's lamb curry. But I liked it. All those different people's containers in our house, in each one a different flavour. All those people that had fed us. Were still feeding us. And the same dishes would pass between us, from one family to another. Sometimes we'd even get one coming back, months later.'

She paused, her eyes now bright with tears. But not the fat heavy soundless tears that just washed her face for weeks and weeks after Dad. These were different, sparkly and sharp, bittersweet. 'You know, I still have an old hummus container with the last bit of daal that my granny ever made. Can't bear to defrost it. But sometimes I open the lid and take a sniff and she's right there again. In her old cardie, which smelled of ginger and had turmeric stains on one sleeve. She loved your Dad. The only one who stuck up for us back then.'

We all took a moment to take in what that meant. We stared at the dish as if it could moo back at us.

'So ...' Taz hesitated. 'What are we going to put in it?'

I opened the fridge and glanced inside, though we all knew without looking how empty it was. Our tiny fridge-freezer was full of instant stuff – nuggets, fries – and there was nothing much in the fridge other than the very basic basics: bread, butter, milk, a hard lump of Cheddar with crusty corners. Mum hadn't cooked anything since Dad and we hadn't wanted to ask her. It was just another little shock on top of the earthquake of loss; Mum had loved cooking and she could rustle up something amazing out of a few leftovers, so every day we got a home-cooked meal after school and thought nothing of it, came to expect it. We had been spoiled in so many ways.

'I could put the Cheddar in the dish. If we just trim off the curly edges?' I said hopefully.

Mum sighed and slowly rose from the chair. She flung open a kitchen cabinet and tutted at seeing a few tins of beans, allowing herself a small nod of satisfaction at the reassuring sight of all her spice jars and packets, still there and waiting. She tore off a sticky note and scribbled on it quickly, handing it to Taz.

'Pop down to Belkis' shop with your sister, no hanging around, come straight back.' And then, seeing our expressions, both me and Taz open-mouthed with surprise: 'Don't expect much. She'll get the leftovers. If there's any. And shut your gobs or you'll stick like that.'

When we got back, Mum banished us to our bedroom and Taz and I lay on our bunk beds, our stomachs rolling as deliciously familiar smells wafted through the flat: onions, coriander, cardamom, ginger, accompanied by the soundtrack of our childhood, chopping, blending, frying, sizzling, until we were drooling into our duvets. When we finally sat down, Mum put our plates in front of us wordlessly. Dad's favourite: chicken biryani, the rice plump and perfect, winking with toasted cumin seeds, the chicken golden brown, glistening with rich gravy and flaked almonds. Taz barely looked up as he began hoovering the entire portion into his mouth, like a human Dustbuster. I took my first mouthful and as each layer of flavour burst on my tongue, tears burst from my eyes. I couldn't help it, but I couldn't stop eating. And as I chewed, I cried. And Mum saw but didn't say anything, just a hand on mine briefly as she poured me some water. And I didn't stop doing either until my plate was empty.

Mum didn't make eye contact with us as she ladled the last of the biryani into the dish with the dancing cows, sealed the top with some silver foil, and pushed it towards me.

'Um ... so shall I just ... leave it on the step, then?'

'If you like.'

'What if someone steals it, though?'

'Not my problem, is it?' Mum was already scrubbing at the rice pan as if it had done something to upset her.

'But ... she won't know why we have—'

Taz nudged me with his bony elbow and shook his head. He was right; there had been enough little miracles today, why push our luck? But I couldn't help it. I did scribble a quick sticky note, which I stuck to the silver foil lid. It said: 'Hello Mrs Daniels. Here's your dish back. And some chicken biryani. Sorry if you're vegetarian. Serena Arif.'

I placed the dish outside the door and knocked on it loudly and dashed inside. I wasn't sure if I could handle a face-to-face encounter. She might shout at me. Or poke me with her banging stick. Or throw the biryani in my face. Or worst of all, not open the door at all and Mum's offering would go cold and mouldy on the balcony, the most public and humiliating of rejections. I waited in the kitchen, even switched off the light, as Mum was now shooing Taz for his shower, and started counting in the dark. One elephant, two elephant … I got to nine when I heard Mrs Daniels' door open and, within two elephants, shut again. I opened our door slowly and stuck my head out. The dish with the dancing cows was gone.

By day four, Mum made out she'd forgotten all about it. She'd certainly been busy: the whole flat had been scoured, scrubbed and polished until me and Taz were getting woozy on cleaning-fluid fumes. The fridge was full again, TV was banned until after we'd done our homework and Mum hadn't even bothered to wash her dressing gown – it had gone straight in the bin.

'How about a trip to Westfield?' Mum said, slipping on her shoes. 'I need a new dressing gown. I'm going to go for something silky this time.'

'And stain-resistant?' I asked.

Mum laughed. She laughed, a proper one, showing her teeth. Taz and I clocked each other and we both started laughing too. We were still laughing when we heard the knock at the door; Mum was still smiling when she flung it open and stared straight into the non-smiling, wrinkled face of Mrs Daniels.

Dad had been right. She was old. Very old, maybe the oldest

person I'd ever seen. There wasn't one bit of her face that wasn't wrinkled, not one hair on her head that wasn't snow white; her hands were like creased papery sheets and her knotted fingers clung onto a steel walking frame against which she leaned heavily, panting slightly. I realised that just getting out of her flat had tired her out. But even though everything about her was ancient, her eyes were bright baby blue, like two sparkly jewels that had fallen into a plate of flour. They stared at Mum and Mum's black flashing eyes stared right back at her. Then Mrs Daniels dipped her chin downwards and, balanced on top of her walking frame, was the dish with the dancing cows. And inside it, eight perfect jam tarts.

'I would have brought 'em round before, but I had to wait for my Tesco delivery,' Mrs Daniels said. Or, rather, wheezed. Her voice was like a slowly opening creaky door. Mum stared at the dish but made no attempt to take it. And then she saw the small card tucked under one of the jam tarts. She squinted at the picture on the front, and then back at Mrs Daniels, realisation dawning. Mrs Daniels nodded.

'Your husband gave it me. I thought you might, you know, want it back.'

Mum took the notelet and opened it, her breath catching as she recognised Dad's distinctive sloping writing inside. Taz and I were behind her, so we could read it too. It said:

> Dear Mrs Daniels, sorry about the noise sometimes. It is hard to keep children quiet all the time. But at least you know we are here if you need us. Anything you want, shopping, chatting, help, just bang on the wall. Loud as you can. And we will come.
>
> Your neighbours, Ayub and Mimi Arif

'I wanted to come – you know, pay my respects that day, but …
well …' Mrs Daniels tailed off croakily.

'The banging on the wall! I thought …' Mum began, then
quieter, 'You were calling us. I didn't know. He never told me.'

Mrs Daniels lifted a veiny hand and placed it briefly on
Mum's arm.

'Lost my husband thirty years ago. Lots he never told me
neither. Loved him to my bones all the same.'

Mrs Daniels eyes dimmed slightly with some old memory
and for a moment, I saw the same shadow, the same wing tip
of my Mum's black crow cross her lined face as she turned
slowly, preparing to leave.

'Mrs Daniels?' Mum said brightly, picking up the dish with
the dancing cows and kicking open the door behind her so
me and Taz had to jump out of the way, 'These look delicious.
Fancy coming in for a cup of tea?'

33 RPM

MARK McLAUGHLIN

We never had our own piano. Each day after school my mother sent me upstairs to practise on our neighbour Mrs Cassidy's. Thirty minutes of Bach and Beethoven, when all I wanted was to be downstairs listening to Bowie and Bolan. Mrs Cassidy met me at the door, milky tea and a thick slice of toast. I'd been warned off accepting these. *Don't be mooching up there.* I tried to turn her down, but she waved me away, wiped her hands on her apron and turned back to the cooker.

I stared at the Holy Picture on her wall; Jesus Christ, his sacred heart aflame, those blue eyes following me. If I gazed at the picture or the rain against the window too long I'd soon be interrupted.

'C'mon now, son,' shouted Mrs Cassidy. 'Keep going!' Her face reddened by the steam rising up from the soup she was stirring. Or I'd hear the *bang! bang! bang!* of my mother's broom from our flat below.

'Tam, you don't realise how lucky you are, son,' my mother said. 'You're the only pupil Miss Edwina sees this side of the park.'

I walked through Kelvingrove and up the hill to Park Terrace for my lessons with Edwina Murray, known to everyone as Miss Edwina. She taught piano to the sons and daughters of Kelvinside's finest. Pinch-nosed and unsmiling, she smelled of Elnett hairspray, polo mints and cigarettes. Her coiffed hair added a good three inches to her height, but she still stood a foot shorter than my gangling teenage frame. Her red-lacquered nails heavily tapped the manuscript when I played my *pianissimo* too loud, my *forte* too quiet. A single gold ring rolled loose on the fourth finger of her right hand.

'Fingers, Thomas!' she cried above the music when I stretched too far or didn't glide over my thumb.

Her black baby grand took up nearly her entire music room. I almost had to edge sideways to get to the stool and wondered how she'd got it in the room. I was afraid to touch the piano at first; my hands might stain the polished wood. A single Mackintosh framed black-and-white photograph of a young couple stood on the piano. He wore a uniform, her dark curls were piled high, bright smiles. A Christmas tree stood in the background as a group of people gathered around them. I had never heard Miss Edwina speak of family, assumed she lived alone, so I wondered if this was her. Each time I stole a glance at the picture her finger tapped rapidly on the side of the piano.

'Once more, Thomas! Once more!'

I was fifteen and those thirty minutes felt like for ever. When the lesson ended I closed her door behind me and at last I was Tam again.

In the weeks leading up to my Grade Three exam, Miss Edwina worked intensively with all pupils, often losing track of time as the lessons ran into one another. The last Monday in October I turned up on time and she told me to wait in the alcove outside her music room. She hurriedly turned on the table lamp and gestured for me to sit down. I listened to someone else's lesson, stared at the wood-panelled walls. There was another picture on the table; the same couple as before, but this time they were dancing, his palm on the small of her back. The edges of the picture were blurred where they had reeled too quickly for the camera. It made them appear almost ghost-like.

I checked the music-room door was closed, and picked up the picture to look more closely. In my teenage clumsiness I misjudged the weight of the frame and immediately dropped it onto the table. My face flushed as I expected the door to open. It remained closed and I picked the picture up again. As I did, I noticed a letter tucked into the back of the frame, the envelope yellowed. It was postmarked 1944, addressed to Miss Edwina. I held it in my hand a moment, began to pull at the letter within, the pages soft and faded. As I held the paper, I became aware that the music had stopped and I hurriedly placed the letter back within the envelope and behind the frame.

After the lesson, I closed the door, pulled my hood up against the autumn wind and headed down the long porch stairs. Already dark outside. I was aware of a light going on in her front room, the curtains in the side window only half drawn. My curiosity maybe raised by the photograph and letter, I edged back up the stairs to peer through the window. Miss Edwina had her back to me, pulling an album from its sleeve. She set the needle and stopped for the briefest moment until the music started, then lit a cigarette and walked towards the window. I stepped back a little but kept looking in. The music was loud enough that it carried into the terrace. It was piano music, of course, but this was different from what she'd taught me. It rang with rhythm, a loose, pounding drummer, deep sliding bass and muted trumpet blasts. The piano glided from bass to treble and back, constantly rolling, at moments almost at a discord with the rest of the music before it was pulled back again. This music sang. This music *moved*. I watched Miss Edwina as she moved too, swaying slightly in time. Her blouse hung loose from her skirt, cigarette in hand. Her shoes kicked free, her stockinged feet slid softly in time across the wooden floor.

She moved closer towards the window and stared out. I thought she was looking straight at me and froze for a moment, but of course the lights from inside were reflecting against the window. She closed her eyes and exhaled cigarette smoke; it rose blue-white around her. Two years I'd gone to lessons, but this felt like the first time I'd seen her, the first time I'd really looked at her face. She stepped forward, closed the curtain and I turned away to hurry home.

That evening, I knelt on the carpet by our record player, going through my parents' albums, playing a little of each track before skipping the needle forward.

'What are you doing, Tam?' asked my mother.

'I heard some music today,' I said. 'I wasn't sure what it was.'

She sat down beside me then, pulled out more of the records as she listened to my description.

'Brass, you say?' she asked. 'Was it something like this?' We both sat quietly, waiting for the needle to work through the initial static as she played me songs by Benny Goodman and Tony Bennett. The light from the electric fire glowed pale orange against her cheeks. I watched how intently she listened to the music. She brought her knees up under her chin, her arms tight around herself. I thought of her singing at family parties, how the shuffle of dancing ceased, glasses held still, cigarettes left to smoke in ashtrays. She was someone else when she sang, no longer just Ma, or Big John's wife.

'How about this?' she asked.

I listened as Sinatra's 'Watertown' began. 'Kinda … it's closer to it … but this music was different.'

As I lay in bed that night I tried to recall the song I'd heard Miss Edwina play, but the memory stayed fuzzy, floating just beyond my grasp. I thought, too, about the photographs of the couple. In my mind there was some great story; he was an RAF pilot and there must have been some tragedy. Fed on comic books, I imagined his Spitfire shot down in a vineyard in France. Grey smoke spiralling up from the fuselage, a broken propeller spinning slowly in the breeze while he lay dead, a picture of Miss Edwina in a locket around his neck. I had an image of her too, in the same field, clutching his last love letter tight against her breast. Stood where her heart got broken, never to be mended, never to be lent again to another man.

The following Monday I forgot my school bag at Miss Edwina's, was crossing Byres Road before I remembered. I hurried back over there. It was five o'clock and fully dark; orange lights shimmered. I rang her bell and stood back from the door. Nothing. As I rang again I realised the door was unlocked and edged slowly inside.

'Hello? Miss Edwina?' The wall clock ticked like a metronome, the weight of its swinging pendulum deep in my belly. I heard the muffled sound of the piano from the music room and moved slowly towards it. I recognised the song immediately from the album I'd heard Miss Edwina play the previous week. It felt melancholic and yet uplifting. The music stopped a moment and I took the opportunity to call her name again. She immediately came into the hallway, her hands moving her hair into shape, checking the straightness of her skirt.

'Thomas, what are you doing here?'

'I'm sorry, Miss Edwina,' I said. 'I rang the bell but there was no answer and the door was open. I left my bag here.'

'Oh … oh, of course.' She opened the door and let me pick it up. A cigarette lay in the ashtray. She hurried past me to stub it out. I pulled my bag across my shoulder, but as I headed for the door I turned round.

'Was there something else?' she asked.

'Yes … I was just wondering what the music was you were playing.'

'The music?' she said. 'Why, it's "Round Midnight". Do you know it?'

'No. But I really liked it,' I said. 'It's just so … so different.'

Her face softened then and she gestured for me to follow her into the front room. She pulled an album from the shelf, held the vinyl up to the light and blew away any dust before she put it on. She handed me the cover: Blue Note Records, Thelonious Monk. I don't remember how long I stayed there, but she played more records for me that evening, both of us sitting in silence, listening, until I remembered my mother would be wondering where I'd got to and made my excuses.

'Oh, of course, Thomas,' said Miss Edwina. 'You must hurry home.'

I never told anyone about that evening and she didn't speak of it again, but as I left she stopped me, her fingers gentle against my forearm.

'Thank you, Thomas.'

Another autumn, this time in Hackney, many years later. I'd taken a call from a solicitors' firm the previous week. I had been difficult to find. When they informed me that I'd been named in Edwina's will, I was taken aback, to say the least. I was sixteen when I'd stopped piano lessons. It's to my shame that I feigned the lessons were impacting on my school exams, when in truth I'd been embarrassed my friends might learn of them. I still remember my mother's face. *Sure, you'll go back once the exams are past.* I had nodded but I never played again.

The box has arrived. I tear it open to find those old records: *Genius of Modern Music, Blue Train, Kind of Blue.* I pull them out, each album older than me but the covers still immaculate. I have these already on CD and MP3, yet somehow these old albums feel different.

I rescue the turntable from the dust of the attic, move the iPhone docking station aside. I sit there while the pink sunset fades to November darkness and a low yellow moon. Just me and those albums. Played so loud I miss my wife calling from her mother's. Played so loud I can barely hear the stop-start engine hum and shuffling moan of traffic through the East End. For the first time in ten years I find myself craving a cigarette. With every bar, every beat, every syncopated snare, rolling piano and blasted horn I am taken. Taken to a world of second lines, yellow spotlights and saxophones. Taken to Minton's Playhouse in Harlem, Copenhagen's Jazzhus, to the hushed darkness of Salle Pleyel, and in some way still I am taken back to Miss Edwina and to Glasgow.

THE DREAMERS

JOHN NIVEN

She looked at the handwritten sign outside Liverpool Street station: 'Hammersmith and City line suspended between Edgware Road and Hammersmith due to local incident.'

She was already tired. She wiped her brow and took a little sip from the Evian bottle, the empty one she'd taken from a desk on the last job and filled from the tap in the staff toilets before she left. (Being careful no one saw her. She'd heard you got into trouble for such things.) It had been a long shift, as they'd asked her to come in early the night before. They were busy at the moment, the cleaning firm. She didn't mind. Another two hours – a few extra pounds to add to the tightly banded roll of blue and brown notes he kept stuffed inside his mattress, in the cut he'd made with the kitchen knife.

Take the tube to Edgware Road and then get the bus?

Or … she saw people already walking down to the bus stop near the station. The 23, she knew, would take her straight to Ladbroke Grove. She put her headphones back in and joined the queue and the bus came right away. She had to stand at first, until a few people got off at Bank, and then she got a seat near the back, by the window. It would be nice to see some of London, especially on such a beautiful morning, already bright and sunny a few minutes after 5 a.m.

She didn't mind the job. There were worse, dirtier things you could be doing. Everyone kept their headphones on and worked away in their own little worlds. She hoovered and she emptied the wastepaper baskets and she dusted and she gathered coffee mugs and washed them out. She liked the last part because it meant going into people's offices, the bigger bosses, and collecting the mugs from windowsills and desks.

She liked to look at the photographs they had on their desks. Of their children and their wives and sometimes their houses and their cars. Along with the other cleaners, she was in and out before the people in the offices knew they were there.

They were there, but they weren't there. Their lives, the people in the offices, were like something out of a film. But she was young, just nineteen. Perhaps her life would turn out good too. Her brother thought so. He was two years older than her and he was the dreamer of the family. He had big plans.

When their parents had been killed, Allah had been merciful enough to leave her big brother. She pictured him, fast asleep in the room they shared. He didn't start work until ten o'clock. He'd got them here, to their uncle, in London. Three years ago now. They'd stayed with relatives, on sofas and floors in Neasden, Harlesden and Collingwood, until their uncle had got them the place they now shared with two others. Four mattresses on the floor in the tiny room. It had been so hot for the last week, up there on the twelfth floor. The window open all the time. Worse for her, trying to sleep in the daytime, when it was even hotter.

Each of them paid £80 a week to the man who owned the flat. There were four people in the other bedroom too.

Eight of them paying the same: hundreds of pounds a week, thousands every month to the man who came to the door to collect the rent. She was proud her brother wasn't like some of the other boys his age from back home. So many of them wouldn't work. They chewed khat all day. Got into fights. Talked about women in a bad way. He wasn't like that. He could be foolish. She knew he sometimes stayed up too late at night, after she left for work, down at his friend Omar's on the second floor, playing on the PS4. It made him tired for work and she nagged him about it. But her big brother had plans.

Their cousins lived down by the sea. In Hastings. Rent was much cheaper down there, although jobs were harder to find than in London. The four of them were saving, going to get a house down there together and try to open a café. She was to have her own room! She couldn't believe it.

She watched the stops go by – St Paul's, Aldwych, Trafalgar Square – as she headed west, listening to Stormzy. Her English was getting better. She'd wanted to enrol in those classes at the community centre, but her brother said they'd want things, papers, things they didn't have. That's what was so good about the plan for Hastings. It would all go in their cousin's name. He was legal.

She rested her head on the juddering glass and fell asleep, dreaming of the sea. Hearing gulls.

Woken by a jolt as the bus came to a stop – a voice saying something over the loudspeakers. She must have dozed off. She still had her headphones on. Looking around, she saw some of the other passengers were angry, slamming down copies of *Metro* and *City AM*, looking up from their phones, talking to each other, which was unusual. Now lots of them were getting up.

She took her headphones out and looked across the road. They were in front of Baker Street tube.

She turned to the lady next to her, a well-dressed woman, white, older than her. 'Is something wrong?' she asked, still sleepy.

'Terminating here,' the woman sighed. Now they could see, up ahead, the road was closed. 'Fire,' someone said. Several passengers shuffling towards the doors were looking at their phones. 'Jesus Christ,' someone else said. She looked over the man's shoulder at his screen. It was a picture of a tower, just like the one they lived in. But it was ablaze. From top to bottom it was just fire.

'Grenfell,' someone said.

She pushed past them and started running.

When she got to Paddington she could see it – wreathed in smoke in the distance, with helicopters circling it. She forced herself to run even harder, even though it already felt like her heart might burst. The pain in her side was helping to drive away the tears. A mantra went through her head: *Please God take me and let him live please God take me and let him live please God ta*— but the photograph on that man's phone, that … nothing could live through that.

She ran – all along Westbourne Park Road, all the way to Portobello, along Lancaster Road. The tears streaming down her face, her throat dry, her legs trembling and buckling under her now, the smoke and the dust in the air getting thicker, and she could hear the helicopters now and the sirens, and the pavements were getting busier until there was a barrier, police cars, and she couldn't go any further.

She could see it – right there. She could see it, but it could not be believed. Just a black, smoking husk now, water still being sprayed into it, steam and smoke billowing from every hole, every window, into the morning sky. It looked like the face of a demon. She collapsed onto the pavement and began sobbing. If he was gone she was on her own, and she could not manage on her own; he was all that she had in the world and all their money would be gone, too, their savings in the mattress, which they had both worked so hard for, and if he was gone she was all on her own and she—

She felt a hand on her shoulder, shaking her gently. She looked up – a policeman. 'Love, are you OK, love?' he was asking her. *We were there, but we weren't there. They will want papers. Things we do not have.* She nodded, trying to breathe in. Trying to stop crying. 'Do you know someone who lives there?' the policeman was asking her now. She decided something.

'My brother. He stays with friends. On the twelfth floor.'

'Hang on,' he said, walking off. A moment passed and he came back. 'Come with me.' They walked off, through the onlookers, through the cordon and along the street, closer to the tower. They turned right towards the sports centre.

There were dozens of people in there. There were mats on the floor, some with people laid on them. Some coughing. The air smoky from their clothes. Sitting on plastic chairs. Sipping cups of water. A lot of people were crying. Outside you were aware of men running everywhere, of shouting and activity and the distant sound of water pumping.

She gave his name to the two women manning a small desk, but they looked through their papers and just shook their heads. When she began to cry again, one of them gave her a hug. They offered her tea, but she didn't like tea. She took a bottle of water and went outside and sat on the step. The fire was out now, but they were still pumping water in, thick smoke billowing out and up into the clear morning sky. Suddenly, for the first time, she thought of their neighbours: the woman with those little children; the old man who lived by the lift …

But the heart is selfish and she thought about her brother again. She realised she had only a single £1 coin and a tube ticket in her pocket and what did this mean? How was she going to live until she was paid next week?

She didn't know how long she sat there, but she was aware of the centre getting busier. More people passing her on the steps. People arriving with food and clothing donations.

People she recognised from the tower, from the lifts and the forecourt, wrapped in blankets, looking dazed, numb, crying. The trestle tables outside the sports centre were soon groaning with boxes of canned food. She was so hungry. Should she speak to someone? *They will want things we do not have.*

Papers. She was so tired, so weak. And then – 'Hey …'

She looked up. He was standing right there. Right in front of her, looking down at her, shielding his eyes from the sun. With the halo of light around him, she thought he might be a dream, like from a film. Until he leaned down and put his hands on her shoulders and said, 'I'm OK.' Then she believed it and she grabbed her big brother and started to cry.

'Shhh. Shhhh …' he said, hugging her.

How? How had he …

'Omar's. PS4,' he said, as if reading her thoughts. 'Look.' He hooked a thumb and forefinger into the pocket of his jeans and pulled it out, just a little bit of the way, careful that no one around could see: the tightly banded roll, the browns and the blues.

'It's OK,' he said. 'It's going to be OK.'

CANNONBALL ASHTRAYS

S. J. THOMPSON

I shook the woman's hand and knew then that everything would be worse. I shook the man's hand, which confirmed it. I was walking out from behind the bar, towel in hand, wiping soap from my cheek.

'Mr Donaghue. We are serving you this notice,' said the woman from the Pubco, holding a notice.

They smelled like company cars and dressed like company-car seats. The man slid a sheet of paper over the bar to me. It soaked up a small pool of white wine as it went, picking up old salt. A dark, crinkly spot appeared under my address. My old address.

'This is my pub,' I said.

'This is no longer your pub,' said the woman.

'You have an hour to pack up. Give us the keys. Every set. And all the final bills and lease documents,' said the man from the Pubco.

'This is my home,' I croaked.

'Home is where the heart is, right?' asked the woman.

'It is,' answered the man.

'Your heart can't be here any more, Mr Donaghue. You'll have to find somewhere else for it.'

'Leave the furniture and appliances. It all counts towards the debt.'

I punched the man in the face. It was the first time in thirty-six years I'd punched anyone. I did not enjoy it. My knuckles hit the flabby skin without a satisfying, movie 'thwack'. He wasn't out cold right away. And he didn't fly through the air either. He saw me coming, turned his head a little and I hit his cheek, knuckle dragging on the cheekbone. There was a weird little scream and his hands went to his face. I took a step forward and punched his nose through his hands. The woman just stood watching. I pushed the man and his body smashed against some tables and stools. I kicked his stomach twice before I felt Kelvin holding me back. The woman grabbed my arm. Kelvin is eighteen now, strong as anything, but a gentle bear. Like his father.

I sat while blood ricocheted around in my veins, until the police led me away. I could hear the Pubco people giving their statements. Making it sound worse than it was. I looked up and there was blood on the right side of the man's face. Maybe it was as bad as they said. I asked Kelvin if he was OK.

'I want to press charges,' said the Pubco man. Kelvin stood by me.

'You go,' I said.

'No, Dad.'

'Go to your mother's. I'll call later.'

I didn't call later. I didn't call for six years.

I left the police station the next morning. They told me I was being sued for damages. Kelvin had dropped off a bag for me. I put it on my back. Couldn't get back in the pub, boarded up with metal sheets and padlocks, so I walked the streets. Didn't stop for about twenty-four hours. Maybe sat on a bench for a bit when my feet pinched but kept walking. And thinking.

Stayed at Patty's house that night. Her husband didn't want me to stay longer and it didn't feel right, anyway. Slept at Ian's the night after, but he said his wife was ill and I had to leave.

'She's ill all right. Mentally fucking ill,' I shouted, and slammed the door.

I visited Mum and Dad's grave and asked them to help out. And I said sorry for being a little shit. And sorry for what I said about Ian's wife.

Where to now? I remembered that time I had an early flight and slept in the airport overnight. Felt so grubby I'd had a stand-up wash in the bathrooms. I went there and slept and washed. Did it for three nights before they recognised me and turned me away from their economy flights and packaged holidaymakers.

I lost the bag in Leeds city centre while sleeping under the stars (hidden above the clouds) on a concrete bench.

'Can you spare some money? So I can get a drink?' I asked a woman at the station.

'This is better,' she said and fished in her bag for a business card. She pressed it into my hand like it was a religious thing.

I took it and put my other hand out to shake hers.

'Don't worry about it,' she said, scurrying off, leaving the hand hanging.

I cried. Looked like a right twat. I haven't asked anyone for money since then. The card was directed at my demographic. Homeless men. The text over-large and comicky. It advertised a free class at the community centre, on the edge of the park. They were teaching skills. Pottery, basket weaving, computers, interview techniques, painting.

I got there early and waited. Some breasts with a big lady behind them turned up with the keys.

'You all right, love?' she asked.

I love it when women call me 'love', but it does make me feel like crying. I didn't cry though. Didn't want to look like a twat again.

'I'm Brendan.'

'Good to meet you. I'm Dhani.'

A few other men arrived. They looked like shit. I put my hand out to Dhani and she shook it. I looked at my hand. There was dirt in the ridges that didn't come out any more.

'Sorry,' I said.

'For what? Come on in now and take a seat. I'll get the kettle on.'

I wanted to cry again because she'd said 'kettle on'.

More men arrived, coughed up from the bits between the streets, looking like carrier bags and corpses. I couldn't talk to them. They all stank. Whisky and piss. I tried to make conversation, but they were stupid on top of it. Most had never read a book, none had ever seen a Scorsese film. One of them said, 'Yes, I watched *Taxi Driver*,' but I dug deeper and found he was thinking of *Caddyshack*.

They all fell into their tasks easy, though; they knew how it worked. This guy over here, it was his turn on the computer first. All the porn sites were blocked, but he tried the URLs anyway before settling in to watch a video on applying make-up for a night on the town. Another guy started drawing and, my God, the picture was amazing. They draped a cloth over a small, round table, put a bowl of fruit, some toy cars and a stack of cans on top, the easel in front. He growled when the others passed because they'd try and grab the fruit. His charcoal drawing looked better than stuff you see in galleries. The guy could hardly speak. I congratulated him and he mumbled shit about a sister and the police, and then he was off again, hand flowing over the paper. Laying down lines with delicate strokes, not overdoing it.

And there were the two guys who just grabbed a teabag and water from the kettle, some chocolate-chip cookies and sat and grunted. Laughing like they knew what the other was saying. I stood near, tried to join in, but there was no way in to their club. There was one other man who sat down and drank tea and cried, spiderweb tats on his sallow face. (Sallow. Not sure that's the right word, must look it up. And spelunking. When I've sorted myself.) Charcoal guy did a little sketch in the corner of his paper, rendering the streaks he saw in the dirt of Tattoo's face. Dhani came to talk to him, but she got nothing. His shoulders rocked, sobbing.

Angela was late, arriving when everyone was into their things. Dhani rolled her eyes. The latecomer was about forty, dressed in black jeans. Afro, short and neat. She wore an Aerosmith T-shirt. Steven Tyler's face had been worn off.

'The car blew up again,' she said.

'It didn't blow up.'

'Who wants to do pottery?' shouted Angela.

'I do,' I said and put my hand up. The only one.

'You don't have to put your hand up, love. You're not in school now.' I love it when women call me 'love'.

'We don't have a wheel any more, but I have some clay. We can shape it with our hands.'

'Like in *Ghost*?' I said.

'Well, yes. Minus the wheel, the dead person and the sexy. Pottery isn't sexy. It's painful, hard and you'll be covered in blood by the end.'

'Really?'

'No.'

She produced some clay from her bag, wrapped in cling film, along with plastic things that looked like scalpels.

'Let's make an ashtray.'

'I did that in school. It was the eighties. Gave it to Mum on Mother's Day.'

'Did she like it?'

'Lung cancer took her, two years after.'

'A cup then. Or a mug. It's like making an ashtray, only the sides are higher. And no one has to smoke anything.'

'I don't smoke.'

Angela left me with the clay and got herself some tea and a cookie. I watched her as I unwrapped the clay.

'Cookie,' I shouted across the room, in Cookie Monster's voice. Was she too young for a *Sesame Street* reference?

'Me love cookie,' she said and crammed the whole thing in her mouth at once. She choked a bit and her eyes watered, but she didn't die, thank God.

As she sipped delicately at her tea, she watched me mould the clay into shape, getting my thumbs down into the corners and willing it into a mug. I was lost in the reverie of creation and she moved off to dole out clay to another. When the basic shape was there, she whispered, 'Well done,' near my ear. It sounded throaty and crumbly. She drank some tea and tried again.

'Your mug is looking almost like a mug. Use the spatula to smooth out the sides. We'll fire it when you're done, in the kitchen oven. And don't forget the handle. Why not try making it decorative?'

I painstakingly fashioned a handle shaped like a question mark, with a scroll and ball on the end. At intervals I would glance up and see if Angela was looking.

'Very inventive!' said Dhani.

Thanks, but I don't care what you think.

One old boy came in late, grabbed an instant coffee and sat himself down to read a book from the tiny library in the corner. Angela interrupted him and they talked for a long time. I willed, with all my will, that she would come over to me again. Then I got engrossed fixing the handle to the mug and gave a little jump when she appeared at my side.

'What's your favourite film?' she asked. 'Eh? I'm going to show a film at the end of next session. I'll get a DVD of something everyone might like.'

'Let me think.'

'Your first answer; just give me it. First thing comes in your head.'

'First thing ...'

'Don't overthink it.'

'*Pretty in Pink*.'

'Wow,' she said. 'Wow. OK. Didn't expect that. I like the song.'

'I was young, it made me cry. What's yours?'

'*The Cannonball Run*. First film my mam took me to see and the last film I watched. I love it. Love it. Love it. If you've not seen it you're in for a treat.'

'I've not seen it.'

'You're in for a treat. I've got a signed poster above my sofa and a guinea pig called Dom DeLuise. Dom DeLuise!'

I said goodbye and left, mug in hand. I felt proud. If Dad was here, he would touch my shoulder and say 'good work'.

I sat in the park admiring the mug and looking at the sky, full of tea and biscuits. Angela walked past. I smiled. She held out her hand, meaning for me to do the same. In my palm she placed a new piece of clay, wrapped in plastic.

'Make something more ambitious. In your own time.'

'I will.'

Over the next month and a bit, I came to the centre (Mondays, Wednesdays and every other Friday when it was open) and did 'pottery' when I could. I learned computer programming with Dhani, tried to do still life in charcoal, and chatted and laughed with Angela, who always returned my smiles. On those days when I was really down, the smile was weak and I think she understood.

One day, she said, 'Hey. I can't go for a drink with people who are technically in my care.'

'What? I didn't …'

'I just quit, Brendan.'

'Oh, I'm sorry.'

'So you're not technically "in my care" any more.'

'I see.'

'And I need a drink.'

'I don't have enough.'

'Don't worry about it, I'll buy.'

We went to the Star and Garter. I felt slightly sick, being in one of those places. We leaned on the bar; she looked relaxed.

'I used to own the Ram.'

'I know. You told me twice,' said Angela.

'Everyone's your friend when you're a landlord. We had trouble, but nothing really bad.'

'What do you want?'

'Another chance to run a pub, to prove I can do it.'

'No, I mean what do you want to drink?'

'Half a Kronie.'

'Two Kronies and two packets of crisps,' she called to the woman serving. 'Any flavour, surprise me.'

'Thanks,' I said.

'Tell me about the pub,' said Angela

'You really want to know?'

'I do.'

'I heard fantastic stories. People tell you everything, and I keep it confidential, like a doctor. Sometimes they throw money at you because they had a good day. "Have one for yourself." It all goes well and then the pub company … they control you, I signed a thing to buy all the beer from them. Then they push up the price. Slowly at first. Like a lobster.'

'Being slowly boiled?'

'Yeah … I think so. Anyway, they jack up the prices, tighten the noose. Rent, rates, all of that. And then swoop in and take it away, every dime. They either reopen with a new patsy or sell the place to developers.'

'How much is a dime?'

'Less than a monkey. That's all I know.'

'Well, yes, I'll bet a pony on that.'

Angela scooped up the beers and I took the crisps. She led the way across the crowded room to a table, where we squatted on short stools and she immediately started peeling the label off her bottle.

'I do that too,' I said.

'So satisfying.'

'I punched the man who took my pub. He wore a dark, grey suit. Hit his face.'

'Violence doesn't help.'

'Son doesn't want to know me, parents dead. Wife is loving seeing me fail. What's your story?'

'Your wife loved you once. I'm sure she doesn't wish you harm.' I felt someone bump into my arm and I froze.

'Sorry, mate!' He laughed like he wasn't sorry, mate. I looked at Angela.

'Have a drink,' she said.

'What about you?'

'Me? From a working-class family. Never had many options but did good at school, did bad at university, didn't give a shit for a while. Got half a teaching qualification and ended up here. After a few shop jobs and filing stuff.'

'Married?'

'Wow, straight in there. OK, this is going to sound awful. Never had a boyfriend. Never anything that lasted longer than one night.'

'What?'

'For realz.'

'I don't believe,' I said, and I didn't.

I opened each of the packets of crisps. 'I want to show you something,' I said.

I took two crisps from the cheese and onion packet and stacked them on top of each other. Then I took two of the BBQ beef crisps and put them on top of the other two. Angela watched me, a four-crisp sandwich in my hand.

'Right,' I said, 'close your eyes.'

'What are you doing?' she asked.

'It's safe. Just close your eyes. Ahhh! Stop peeking. Close them.'

'OK'

'Now I want you to imagine the Empire State Building. Know what it looks like? Been to New York?'

'Yes. What is this?'

'Just wait. Imagine the building, all tall. Standing there. Chrysler Building just behind it, off to the left, I think. Sounds of taxis honking their horns. Go down a bit towards the street. Pan the camera down. Smoke coming off the manhole in the road, people milling about. The lights of some shows on Broadway. Times Square, all lit up. It's night time now.'

'OK, I see it,' she said.

'Just imagine it. I'm putting these crisps in your hand. Got them?'

'Yep.'

'Picture the lights, the people. Shops, diners, smoke, chefs frying onions, big, tall shakes. Oreo flavour.'

'You're making my mouth water.'

'Slices of apple pie, cream.'

'I see it all. I can see it clear.'

'Put the crisps in your mouth and chew slowly. It's a New York cheeseburger. Mustard, mayo, thick cheese, juicy, red meat.'

I placed the crisps in Angela's hand and she put them into her mouth. She let them sit on her tongue a moment, then her lips closed and she chewed.

'Oh my God!' she whispered.

'You can taste it? Taste the burger in your mouth?'

She opened one eye. 'Tastes like cheap crisps,' she laughed and carried on chuckling to herself.

'Thanks.'

'I'm joking. I tasted the burger. I did, I saw it on the plate in front of me. And it tasted like burger in my mouth. Honest, it worked.'

'Good,' I said slowly.

'Don't you sign on?' she asked.

'Yeah, I did while I was allowed to. Used the address of my pub. They left the post on the step, I snuck up and took it.'

'"Snuck" isn't a word.'

'I think ... maybe it is.'

'Snook is the word you were looking for.'

'"Snorked." Anyway, no one was living there for ages. Even when there was, I never hurt or even scared anyone. I wouldn't hurt anyone, except when I did.'

'I sense that. You are a good man, Brendan. That's the vibe I get.'

'Why do you do the job you do?' I asked.

'I enjoy it,' she said. 'And I'm good at it.'

I went to the centre the next day, half expecting to see Angela. Some soppy-looking thing was in her place. The thing cocked her head to one side and smiled pityingly as I walked in.

'I'm doing pottery,' I said.

'Oh, sorry. We don't do that here,' she whined. 'But I can teach you how to send an email.'

I still went to the community centre as often as I could. Never missed a session. Toby, who did the charcoal, opened up one day and told me about his squat. Said there might be room for me. Sharing with ten other blokes in a massive six-bedroom house. Best place I ever lived. The water ran and the toilet flushed and I found a good mattress. Firm, yet just soft enough. And generally they were all good people. I never saw one proper fight there.

I bumped into Angela on a Saturday, three months after she left. It was in the Bluebird shopping centre; she was there with her mum. I was looking at the Xbox games when she said, 'Hey!' behind me.

'I was thinking about you,' she said.

'You were?' I said. 'You sure about that?'

'Yes, wondering what you were doing now. That kind of thing. Oh, and this is my mum, Chardonnay. Chardonnay, this is Brendan. I taught him to make a mug.'

'Pleased to meet you,' I said.

'Likewise,' she frowned.

'Chardonnay is a name I usually hear on younger women,' I said to the wrinkled old prune.

'Mum changed her name. By deed poll,' said Angela.

'Well, I won't ask what it was before,' I said.

'I'm going to take the weight off,' said Chardonnay, and hobbled over to a yellow, plastic seat.

'I made something with the clay you gave me.'

'I'd like to see that.'

'If you go for a drink with me, I could bring it and show you. It's at the squat.'

'How's that working out?'

'Pretty good.'

'I don't know about a drink.'

'I can pay this time. Got a bit of cash, clearing a building site for a few days. I can actually buy a drink.'

Chardonnay was glaring at me from the hot, yellow plastic.

'I don't think I can, Brendan,' said Angela.

'What's up? You seeing someone? Just a friendly drink is all.'

'I'm not. Typically, I am not. I'm also enjoying not seeing anyone.'

'It's not a date, it's a friendly drink.'

Angela took one step back and her eyes traced a line around me. 'OK.'

'Dog and Duck, tomorrow at eight.'

'Thursday. At seven.'

'Done.'

Angela was already sitting with a beer when I arrived. I walked in and she laughed.

'What?' I smiled. 'What's with the laughing?'

'Your hair! It's neat, and brushed. You trimmed your beard and your ears. You look good. Let me look at your hands. Yep, clean too. New shirt.'

'Yeah, about that. I can afford two Cokes and that's about it. Found the shirt and trousers—'

'Oh yeah, nice new chinos.'

'At the charity shop.'

'I'm doing well in my new job,' she said. 'I'll get us both a beer.'

I watched her go to the bar. She turned back to look at me as she waited. Gave me a wink and smile. I felt something in my heart ache. Stupid. It was gone before she got back.

'What's the new job, then? Chief potter for Wensleydale?'

'You know that's a cheese, right? You mean Wedgwood?'

'Yeah, I mean Wedgwood.'

'Funnily enough, you're almost there. I am now part owner of a shop where people can make their own crockery and paint it and glaze it and get a coffee or cake too. The cakes are amazing. I brought you some.'

She fished in her bag for a plastic takeaway box with cake in it. I took a sip of beer.

'You don't need to give me food. I'm doing OK.'

'It's not pity. It's friendly. If you don't see it that way, I can go now.'

I must have sounded like a dick.

'Thank you.'

'And you said you had something for me,' she said.

'You know that Lionel Richie video?'

'What?'

'I thought of making your head in clay. I gave it serious, serious thought and then realised that A: I wouldn't be able to make it well enough to be flattering.'

'True.'

'And B: it's a little creepy. No matter how well intentioned.'

'Well done for not going the creepy route. You didn't go the creepy route, did you?'

'You told me about Dom DeLuise, your guinea pig. Well, I made Dom in clay.'

'Show me!'

I lifted the Waitrose carrier bag onto my lap and retrieved the Dom Deluise-shaped lump of clay from within.

Angela stared at it, turning it round in her hand, looking from every angle. 'Oh. My. God.'

'You like it?'

She looked at the clay then looked at me, right in the eyes, a smile growing on her face. I didn't look away.

ABOUT THE AUTHORS

Susan E. Barsby lives in Nottingham with her husband and young daughter. By day she works in communicaions and by night she writes novels, short stories and creative non-fiction. Her work has been published in *The A3 Review*, *DNA Magazine* and *Paper and Ink Zine*, among others. She can be found on Twitter at @SusanEBarsby.

Joel Blackledge has been a teacher, bartender, pot-washer, historian, transcriber, cameraman, furniture salesman, and for one day he was a lumberjack. Now he's mostly a writer and filmmaker. His fiction has been performed at the monthly literary event Liars' League, and his writing on cinema appears in publications including *Little White Lies* and *Bright Wall/ Dark Room*. His films have played at international festivals from Kingston to Alaska, and are also available online.

Christopher Brookmyre is the author of twenty-one crime and science fiction novels, including *Black Widow*, winner of the 2017 Theakstons Old Peculier Crime Novel of the Year. His work has been adapted for stage, television, radio and even a video game. His most recent book is *Places in the Darkness*.

Daisy Buchanan is an author and journalist who frequently contributes to a wide range of magazines and newspapers, and appears on TV and radio. Her latest book, *How to Be a Grown Up*, a memoir about surviving your mistakes, is published by

Headline. Daisy was *Grazia* magazine's agony aunt, a role she practised for in her first job, at the teen magazine *Bliss*, and as the eldest of six sisters. She lives by the seaside.

Joanna Campbell is a full-time writer from the Cotswolds. Her short-story collection, *When Planets Slip Their Tracks*, is published by Ink Tears and was shortlisted for the 2016 Rubery Book Award and longlisted for the 2017 Edge Hill Story Prize. Her novel, *Tying Down The Lion*, is published by Brick Lane Publishing. Her stories appear in all kinds of magazines and anthologies and she was the winner of the 2015 London Short Story Prize. Her novella-in-flash, *A Safer Way to Fall*, was published this year by the Bath Flash Fiction Award.

L. A. Craig's fiction appears online and in anthologies *Jawbreakers*, *Scraps*, *An Earthless Melting Pot* and *To Carry Her Home*. She was longlisted for Fish Publishing's Flash Fiction Prize, the Bristol Short Story Prize and was a finalist in the Words with Jam Bigger Short Story and National Flash Fiction Day competitions. She received a Northern Writers' Award in 2014 and was a finalist in BBC Radio 4's *Opening Lines*; her story 'Flour Baby' was broadcast in 2015. Her short play *Metal Sandwich* was performed in 2017 at Live Theatre in Newcastle. She is currently writing a children's novel.

Kat Day is a writer, teacher and mum to two brilliantly rambunctious daughters. She has written non-fiction articles for various publications and contributed a chapter to the book, *The Secret Science of Superheroes*. 'We Have Now' will be one of her first published stories; she also has a piece of flash fiction in the online magazine *Daily Science Fiction*. She is incredibly proud to be able to support the *24 Stories* project and hopes the book makes everyone who reads it smile. You can follow her on Twitter at @chronicleflask and read more of her work at thefictionphial.wordpress.com.

Barney Farmer writes drunken bakers and similar for *Viz*. Uses biro. No longer trading as rap act Poundmaster Plus but retains all copyright. Name available for lease or hire.

John Fidler has been messing about with words since before his birth – OK, maybe a bit after that: lyrics for unsuccessful indie bands, lots of junk mail during his career in advertising (it's nothing like *Mad Men*), a string of unstarted novels and far more tweets than can surely be healthy. But, unless you count two letters in the same issue of *Smash Hits*, this story is the first time he has been published. He is quite chuffed about it and might even get his finger out and write some more.

Yasmina Floyer lives in London where she takes care of her family and works as a private tutor. After completing an MLitt in creative writing at Glasgow University, her poetry has appeared in *By&By Poetry*, her short fiction has appeared in *Avis Literary Journal*, *Litro Magazine*, *Doppelganger Magazine* and in Bridge House Publishing's 2017 short-story anthology, and a personal essay has appeared in *Shooter Magazine*.

Mike Gayle, a former journalist and agony uncle, is the author of thirteen novels including the *Sunday Times* bestseller *My Legendary Girlfriend*. His latest novel, *The Man I Think I Know* (Hodder and Stoughton) is out now. He is based in Birmingham. @mikegayle

Julian Gyll-Murray decided to become a writer as soon as he learned how to read. After years spent selling chocolates in Brussels and teaching English in Bangkok, Julian now works in London as a schoolteacher and playwright. He is the winner of both the Words Just Words Science Fiction prize of 2012 and the Save As Shakespeare Prize of 2013, and has seen his fiction printed in numerous collections, including *BFS Horizons#2*, *Endless Darkness Vol. 2* and *History Will Be Kind*.

J. L. Hall is a Scottish lecturer in the creative industries and is currently working on her second novel. She is proud to be an own-voices writer; she lives with PTSD. In 2016, she was a finalist in the Flash 500 Novel Opening Chapter and Synopsis Competition, Impress New Writers Prize, and Lucy Cavendish College Fiction Prize. Her piece on trauma and recovery is included in the forthcoming *A Wild and Precious Life* anthology. She lives in London with her partner, and she tries to balance life, work and writing with the 24/7 challenges of PTSD. www.jlhallwriter.com

Paul Jenkins has been employed by a large number of organisations in a wide range of positions. He no longer has a CV, preferring to carry a redacted *Yellow Pages* around instead. A typical Aquarius, with an increasing collection of phobias, he can be found singing lewd sea shanties in the many abandoned funfairs of South Wales.

A. L. Kennedy was born in Dundee in 1965. She is the author of nineteen books: seven literary novels, one science fiction novel, one children's book, seven books of short stories and three non-fiction volumes. She is a Fellow of the Royal Society of Arts and a Fellow of the Royal Society of Literature. She has twice been amongst those in the Granta Best of Young British list. She is a member of the Akademie Der Kunst. She is also a dramatist for stage, film, TV and radio. She writes for a number of newspapers in the UK and further afield. Her prose is published in a number of languages and she has won a number of national and international awards, including the Costa Prize, the Austrian Stat Prize for International Literature and the Heinrich Heine Prize. She has worked as a stand up comedian and occasionally writes and performs one person shows.

Mark McLaughlin was born in Glasgow. He now lives in east London with his partner and two children, where he balances family life, work, studying for an Open University degree and writing short stories. Mark is currently working on his first novel.

Pauline Melville's first collection of short stories won the *Guardian* Fiction Prize, the Commonwealth Writers' Prize and the MacMillan Silver Pen award. She went on to win the Whitbread Prize, the Guyana Prize for Literature and an accolade from the New York Public Library. She lives in London.

John Niven was born in Irvine, Ayrshire. He is the author of *Kill Your Friends*, *The Amateurs*, *The Second Coming*, *Cold Hands*, *Straight White Male* and *The Sunshine Cruise Company*.

Dan Rebellato is a playwright and his work for stage and radio includes *Here's What I Did With My Body One Day*, *Static*, *Chekhov in Hell*, *Cavalry*, *Emily Rising* and *My Life Is a Series* *of People Saying Goodbye.* He recently completed an award-winning 27-episode adaptation of Zola's 'Rougon-Macquart' novels for Radio 4 under the title *Emile Zola: Blood, Sex & Money.* He is also Professor of Contemporary Theatre at Royal Holloway University of London.

Nina Stibbe is the author of four books. Her contribution to this collection is a true story. She was born and raised in Leicester, then lived in London for twenty years, and now lives in Cornwall. She holds a full driving license and co-owns a small dog.

Meera Syal, CBE, is an acclaimed actor and writer of stage and screen. She is the author of *Anita and Me, Life Isn't all Ha Ha Hee Hee* and *The House of Hidden Mothers.*

S. J. Thompson is a writer and video producer from London, the home of Danger Mouse. In his spare time he writes stories and creates comics. When he needs inspiration, he walks his dog and when he doesn't need inspiration, he still walks the dog because the dog always needs walking.

Zoe Venditozzi's first novel, *Anywhere's Better Than Here*, won the *Guardian*'s Not the Booker prize and was also shortlisted for the Dundee International Book Prize. She has just completed a new novel about psychic phenomena and dark domesticity and is working on a collection of short stories. Zoe lives in Scotland with her husband and three children.

Irvine Welsh is a writer, usually of fiction, who lives mostly in Miami Beach.

ABOUT THE AUTHORS

Murray Lachlan Young's poetry career began in the underground cabaret nights of mid-nineties London. He is now best known as an 'across network' performer on BBC radio, appearing regularly on BBC Radio 4's *Saturday Live*, Radio 5 Live and *Test Match Special*. Since 2011, Murray has been resident poet at BBC Radio 6 Music. Murray has two sons and lives in London.

ACKNOWLEDGEMENTS

Rhona: Love and thank you to Dad (John) for his love, patience and belief in me; Jeanie Taylor for her loving kindness; to Dr Frank Corrigan for his broad and expert mind and Terence Dackombe for his sage advice.

Big love to my fellow members of the 'fab four' who, combined, helped create magic: Paul Jenkins aka 'book Dad' for his literary passion and determination, what an adventure this turned out to be, eh?! Kath Burke for believing in our idea, her advice and great chats. And to Steve for making every step of the book's progress look so beautiful and for coaxing me back down to earth whenever I needed it!

Paul: I would like to thank Zoe and Martha for their support, encouragement, cups of tea and tolerating my stressing, panicking and general fretting; my mum and dad for their advice, love and values; thanks to Martin Gordon, Maria Donovan and Rob Middlehurst – these three people planted the idea in my head that I might have a talent for writing and so must take the blame for my scribblings earlier in this book. Without Steve Thompson, this book wouldn't look nearly as great as it does … and finally, an enormous thank you to Kathy Burke. Her selflessness, patience and enthusiasm for this project has been the difference between me and Rhona discussing our idea on social media about maybe writing a book and that book actually being written. And finally to Rhona. We've fought and argued and raged and laughed and generally done all you can do without ever having met. We did it.

Paul, Rhona, Steve and Kath would collectively like to thank all at Unbound, particularly John Mitchinson, Philip Connor, Anna Simpson, Becca Day-Preston and DeAndra Lupu for their belief in the project from the beginning, their enthusiasm, guidance, encouragement and for giving this book physical form; Nick Pettigrew and John Rain for sharing their contacts; Channel 4's *The Last Leg* team for allowing Kathy to rocket launch the project; Jo deBarr for her sharp eyes; Sian and Shiraz from Trauma Aid UK for all their kindness and help; the board of Trauma Response Network for their warmth and enthusiasm; Ross Wilkie and Laura Moore for their assistance; and finally, to everyone who submitted a story to this project.

SUPPORTERS

Unbound is a new kind of publishing house. Our books are funded directly by readers. This was a very popular idea during the late eighteenth and early nineteenth centuries. Now we have revived it for the internet age. It allows authors to write the books they really want to write and readers to support the writing they would most like to see published.

The names listed below are of readers who have pledged their support and made this book happen. If you'd like to join them, visit: www.unbound.com.

@BooksandJohn
30 day
All our kids at A Life Explored
Maria Adams
Keith Adsley
Adrian Ainsworth
Dolly Alderton
Rona Allan
Chris Allen
Julia Anderson
Marie Andrews
Ebba Aquila
Afroze Asif
Sophie Aslett
Michael Atkinson

Sharla Attala
Steve Ayland
Karen Badenoch
Sam Bain
Aidan Baker
Simon Barsby
Susan Barsby
Morven Beagan
Stephen Bell
Garry Bennett
Melanie Bewers
Dave Beynon
Susmita Bhattacharya
Brian Bilston
Ryan Bird

Nicholas Blake
David Bleicher
Margaret Bluman
Polly Bolshaw
Susan Booth
Adam Boult
Sarah Boundy
Priscilla Bowden
Lorna Bowman
Anne Boyle
Katharine Bradbury
Lauren Bravo
Ed Broughton
Sarah Brown
Lilian Bryce-Perkins
Elaine S. Bryceland
Kate Buchan
Helen Bull
Mark Burgess
Adrian Burns
Tanvir Bush
SJ Butler
Carl Butterworth
Polly Butterworth
Catherine Byrne
Janis Cairns
Remembering Calum Downes
Adrian Campbell
Caitlin Campbell
Georgia Campbell
David Carr
Jeff Chapman
Christopher Chimonas

Neil Claxton
Sharon Clayton
Steve Clough
Anthony Coates
Bernadette Coates
Ruhina Cockar
Mal Collins
Tim Collins
Sarah Cooper
Tamsen Courtenay
Rebekah Cowan
Russell Cowper
Lisa Craig
Tayler Cresswell
Emma Captain Croad
Julia Croyden
Danielle Culling
Gill Cummings
Paula Curd
Terence Dackombe
Elodia Dalmonte
John David
Alan Davies
Melissa Davies
Clea Davis
Louise Davis
Stephen Day
Jo deBank
Emily Dewhurst
Sharon Dominey
Sandie Donnelly
Emma Douglas
Michele Douglas

Tiernan Douieb
Carolyn Drake
Jan Droge
Meredith Dryden
Gordon Duncan
Rod Dykeman
Yvonne Dykes
Julia Edwards
Nicola Edwards
Sarah Edwards
Elaine, Richard and Alex
Karen Elizabeth
Jennie Ensor
Wendy Errington
Benedict Evans
Dr Shane Ewen
Patricia Eyles
Robert Luis Faria
Marie Ferguson
John Fidler
Lisa FitzKenna
Rebecca Flaherty
Ana Fletcher
Meredith Follett
Eamonn Forde
Anna Foster
Hilly Foster
Sally Fowler
Becky Fox
Lisa Fransson
Isobel Freeman
G.L.O.R.I.A! G.L.O.R.I.A!
Elly-Mae Gadsby

Symington Gail
Ter Gallagher
Andrew Gardner
Hannah Gibbons
Alison Gibbs
Joyce Gibson
Mark Gillies
Rebecca Gransden
Martyn Grant
Phil Greenland
Amy Gregson
Cathie Grice
Conor Gunn
David Gyll-Murray
Julian Gyll-Murray
Ann-Katrin Hahn
Zen Hameed
Katharine Harding
Paula Hardy
Nick Harleigh-Bell
Jo Harper
Juliet Harris
Ines Harrison
Lauren Harrison
Hannah Hawken
Abbie Headon
Billy Heal
Nicky Herriot
Tania Hershman
Donna Hindley
Jason Hoffmann
Rachel Holland
David Holmes

Claudia Howard
Heather Hughes
Stephanie Hutton
Tania Irvine
Graeme Jarvie
Gareth Jenkins
Lisa Jenkins
Martin Jenkins
Paul Jenkins
Sam Jennings
Jacqui Jones
Sian Jones
Tracey Jones
Angus Jordan
Kathryn Kaupa
James Kemp
Christina Kennedy
Paul Keogan
Hannah Kershman
Steve Kesterton
Dan Kieran
Patrick Kincaid
Shane Kirk
Kevin Kitt
Kirsty Koeswoyo
Carina Krause
Lynsey Leaver
Gayle Letherby
Gillian Logie
Lozzi xx
Adam Lumb
Bobbie Allen MacNiven-
    Young

Lisa Maguire
Felicity Maiden
Linda Mannheim
Eddie Marshall
Jessica Martin
John Martin
Paul Martin
Zoe Martin
Sarah Massara
Christine Matthews
Suesan Matthews
Andrea Mayer
Cormac McConnell
Rebecca McCormick
Miranda McCoy
Margot McCuaig
Jon McGill
Malcolm McGowan
Maria McGrath
Brian McGuinness
Lucie McKnight Hardy
Liam McLaughlin
Mark McLaughlin
Rachel McMaster
Kirsteen McNish
Janet McQuade
Bennett Mcveigh
Helen Milburn
Mandy Miller
Kathryn Millington
Emma Milne-White
Helen Miskin
Jessica Mitchell

Paul Mitchell
Russell Mitchell
John Mitchinson
Lucy Moffatt
Jackie Monte-Colombo
Danielle Moore
Gareth Moore
Sian Morgan
Anne-Marie Jane Morrison
Tim Morrison
Hannah Moulder
Mary Mount
Flora Mountford
Mum and Dad
Charlotte Mumford
Bobby Murdoch
Janet Murphy
Alona Murray
Bernadette Murray
Carlo Navato
Jill Neilson
Rich Nelson
James Newell
Jeanne Nielsen
Sarah Niles
Ian Norris
Nina Nouripanah
Jack O'Donnell
Marina O'Loughlin
Maria Manchester O'Malley
Kieran O'Shea
Sonya Oates
Laura Ogryzko

Evonne Okafor
Viv and Andy Oliver
Emily Orlowski
Sally Osborn
Annika Osborne
Gabrielle Osrin
Rachel Page
Mélanie Boyer Panagi
James Craig Paterson
Stevie Pattison-Dick
Chantal Patton
Simon Phillips
Grace Plant
Justin Pollard
Simon Price
Rachael Prior
Sarah Proudlove
Jo Pymer
Sean Quigley
Roger Quimbly
Tom Rafferty
Irene Ramsay
Olive Rayner
Dan Rebellato
Sandra Reid
Victoria Richards
Helen Richardson
Mihai Risnoveanu
Jane Roberts
Frances Robinson
Steve Rowling
Janet Ruddock
Melissa Rule

Mark Rutterford
Helen Rye
Elizabeth Rosalind Rymer
Shanine Salmon
David Sargen
Louise Savage
Matthew Savine
Jenny Schwarz
Mike Scott Thomson
Madeleine Severin
Lucy Shaw
Lisa Marie Shepherd
Hannah Sheppard
Viv Shilton
Helen Shiner
Glen Simmers
Geoff Simpson-Scott
Deborah Sims
Maureen Sloan-Griffiths
Donna Smith
Julia Smith
Nick Smith
Julie-ann Squires
Alex Stabler
Peter Stacey
John Stansfield
Henriette B. Stavis
Liz Street
Tristan Swales
Dave Sweetin
Paul Sweetman
Christine Sydney
T C

Susan Tang
Bridget Leggy Tanner
Jeanie Taylor
Lorna Taylor
Ruth Taylor
Alison Telfer
Anne Theobald
Celeste Thomas
Collette Thomas
Sophie Thompson
Steve Thompson
Clare Tinston
Sabine Totemeyer
Catriona Troth
Wendy Tuxworth
Jo Unwin
Maggie Vaughan
Anna Vaught
Mark Vent
Helen Verity
Natasha Viner
Johanna von Fischer
Jo W
Rankin Waddell
Jonathan Wakeham
Melissa Wallis
Gareth Watkins
Angela Watt
Gemma Waughman
Anna Wharton
Hannah Whelan
Johanna White
Margaret White

Ross Wilkie
Cheryl Willers
Hannah Williams
Holly Williams
Jen Williams
Rebecca Williams
Rose Williams
Catherine Williamson
Kate Winstanley
Laura Woods
Debbie Wythe
Tobi Yasin
Jodi Young
Chris Yuillk